Tender WARRIORS

Tender WARRIORS

a novel by

Rachel Guido deVries

Firebrand
Books
Ithaca, New York

This book may not be reproduced in whole or in part, except in the case of reviews, without permission from Firebrand Books, 141 The Commons, Ithaca, New York 14850.

Book and cover design by Mary A. Scott
Cover illustration © by Cathy C. Harris
Typesetting by Martha J. Waters (Cornell Daily Sun)

Printed on acid-free paper in the United States of America by McNaughton & Gunn

This publication is made possible, in part, with public funds from the Literature Panel, New York State Council on the Arts.

Library of Congress Cataloging-in-Publication Data

deVries, Rachel Guido, 1947-
   Tender warriors.

   I. Title.
PS3554.E9284T46 1986 813'.54 86-4690
ISBN 0-932379-15-X (alk. paper)
ISBN 0-932379-14-1 (pbk. : alk. paper)

For my Mother and Father

acknowledgments

I began *Tender Warriors* in November of 1981. The book was written in two places—Cazenovia, NY, where I make my home, and Provincetown, MA, where I have spent a great deal of time. Along the way, many people helped me, and I want to thank them: Dennis Campbell, Sue Dove Gambill, Pam Genevrino, Mary Green, Joan H. Freeman, Rita Hammond, Ellen Jaffe, Rhoda Lerman, Gerri Mace, Lana Paolillo, Jo Hunt Piersma, John B. Rappise, Lorri Rappise, Rita Rappise, Marian Roth, Barbara Smith.

A special thanks to Lynne Negele, R.N., for her help with the medical research; to P.E. McGrath, whose financial and moral support during the revisions of this book mean a great deal to me; to Nancy K. Bereano, with whom working has been a real pleasure; to Priscilla Van Deusen, who understood the spirit of *Tender Warriors* right from its start, and who loves Sonny DeMarco. And I especially thank my mother and father, who have taught me how to love, how to fight, and how to survive.

author's note

I had great dreams as I wrote this book. One of the dreams was about St. Lucy, and as I read about her life, I found her described as a tender warrior. The book's title was born then, and other connections also make their way into the lives of these characters. Lucy, of Syracuse, Sicily, lived during the third century and is a saint often invoked for help with diseased or failing eyesight. Lucy's appearance in my dreams and in *Tender Warriors* was a bit of a surprise, but I was raised Catholic and Italian — in an atmosphere of both religion and a wonderful kind of spirituality that is, I think, closer to magic than anything else.

Rachel Guido deVries
Cazenovia, New York
21 January 1986

one

THIS MUCH HE KNEW for sure: he was damned if he was going to let anybody — not even his father — stop him from getting by. Seven months had passed since they had the fight and he had left, or been thrown out, depending on how you wanted to look at it. And he was getting by, earning a living and learning a trade, if you could call being a short order cook at the QuikStar a trade.

Sonny DeMarco glanced at the clock; not the one over the greasy counter in the Star but across the street, the lit-up clock of Syracuse Savings Bank on Salina Street. He worked the 3-11 shift in a seedy section of the city where the ghouls and the hookers and the junkies warmed up or broke between tricks or fixes or petty deals. He had three hours to go, and he was a little tired of standing behind the counter seeing things that brought back too many memories, or leaning on his elbows on the red counter top, drinking too much coffee or eating too much greasy food to stop thinking. He was a big man, more in girth than height. He stood about 5'10" and weighed 250 easy, and in the last seven months he had quit being so meticulous about things like shaving or taking a shower. He knew it. He just couldn't quite see the point of it. He was always a little tired or preoccupied, always trying to feel again, to feel enough to make some sense of the life he was without a doubt living. But he was living it on the surface of his skin, not quite in it, not quite ever fully in one place. Back and forth he went in memory, in time, always a little foggy, always once or twice removed from the way he knew he used to feel, and still over everything he did or thought or saw or felt was a yellow and tender ache of sadness, old and familiar and full of longing.

Sonny looked at the seven or eight people scattered in the QuikStar. None of the regulars were here yet: it was too early, but the drunks were beginning to straggle in, and in one booth were two white women not more than seventeen or eighteen, with a Black guy, drinking coffee. At the counter another white girl sat alone, again young, her eyes hard and glittery, empty, reminding him of the fish he used to catch up north; her skin was bad, yellowish — the sallowness and fine pimples like a rash dotting her face, looking pitiful in the dingy and unnatural fluorescent lights that hung, two tubes suspended between the counter and the grill. He stood there cooking in old grease, pouring always stale coffee from the glass carafes mottled with cooking oil. He could see that in some way he fit in here, where everyone was lost. The Quik-Star was safe, an oasis in everyone's desert, and his heart ached in the bowl of his chest like a pure white bird, fragile and tender. He felt the ache, knew it about himself, looked around him, looked at the customers in the mirror that hung over the booths and thought, maybe I do belong here. I come from this, like with his sister Lorraine.

He can only vaguely remember when they found out about Lorraine. Eighteen years ago already, the night they brought her home. The cops brought her in, she was sixteen, the cops brought her instead of throwing her in jail because they knew his father. The needle marks, the set of works they pulled out of her purse. He remembers her face, too calm, but her eyes were screaming. His father's rage, how he beat her, then made his mother and his oldest sister put Lorraine in the tub.

His sister Rose tried to stop the old man, and he threatened to kill her. Sonny couldn't remember where he stood, what he did. Later, Rose tried to talk to him, but he couldn't talk. Lorraine took off the next day; he had only seen her a few times since. He hadn't seen Rose since he left home. Or his Momma. Sometimes he thought of calling Rose. A mess, he thought, no different from this place.,

It was just about eight o'clock, and at eight at the QuikStar the winos and old drunks came tumbling in, close as they were to the mission soup kitchen. They came in for coffee afterwards; Sonny thought it was funny how they kept that social habit, dinner and coffee. Soup and coffee. After dinner you always have coffee and a cigarette. Talk about the weather if it's snowing. Talk about Thunderbird or Ripple or Paisano Red if you're feeling flush. Talk about the best streets to pick up some change. All the same. When there was home they talked about the lasagna or the stuffed braciole. The artichokes. The meatballs. Or his father'd talk about the war, or how hard he worked. All of them around the table on Sundays at one, right after church, or on the holidays with all the aunts and the cousins. He could never eat the meatballs.

He remembers how his father tried to force him to eat the meatballs. But he had seen his Momma make them. The chop meat like a mound of pale worms, the raw eggs added like someone's confused eyes, the wettened bread, the sound as she squished it together. The sound always made him sad. He was only four or five or six at first, and his father never stopped forcing them on him. Both of his sisters laughed their betrayal. They ate the meatballs, they always laughed. Sometimes he tried to laugh with them; it was not the same laughter.

He finished his shift at eleven. He was relieved by Moses O'Toole, a skinny Black man not long out of the hospital. He doesn't know how old Moses is and Moses doesn't know how old Sonny is. It is all confused because Sonny is twenty-seven and looks like he could be well into his thirties, and Moses is forty and looks like he's pushing sixty.

There was something the two men liked about each other. Something simple. Moses put it this way to himself: "That Sonny don't poke his big guinea nose in nobody's business." Moses also liked the way Sonny was polite, even to the hookers and the winos, who were the rudest, bad-assed ones come in the Star. Moses thought Sonny's Momma must of taught him good, like his Momma did once a long time ago. When Moses had gone in the hospital and had a tumor removed from his lung, and the bored white intern told him a bunch of stuff he couldn't make out, something about x-rays and getting it all and how he had to stop smoking, Sonny came to see him, clean shaven and smelling of soap and Old Spice, and tried to talk to the intern for Moses cause Sonny could see something wasn't right there.

Sonny knew because he'd been in the hospital plenty of times growing up. First, for his big head. Water on the brain, his Momma had told him when he was twelve and she thought he could understand. How they had got it all, or it stopped itself and his head wouldn't get any bigger now. But still he had a lot of infections. Once he almost died from it because it turned into meningitis and he rocked all night in a kind of blurred agony while his Momma tried to give him a bath and a shot of whiskey. He'd been eighteen. That time was the worst, and he still got bad headaches. He knew his Momma worried so he called her at least once a month from a phone booth.

He was getting a headache tonight as he checked out to Moses. Moses was ten minutes late, came in making a joke about getting laid, but Sonny knew it was the coughing again that kept him out. He liked how Moses never complained, instead asked Sonny if he had another headache. Moses could always tell because when Sonny had a headache he looked down a lot, like raising up his eyes to the fluorescent light hurt him, and it did. It hurt him, and something about the light touched memory, sensation, pushed Sonny again to the inside, straight to his heart, slow and keen, making time shift, the present and the past and some hazy notion of the future filled with melancholy. And sometimes lately it was also tinged with anger and loss and mourning and a sense of being remote, apart, that he could not quite understand, though he recognized it.

He was eight, skinny then, his head too large. He didn't know why the kids called him egghead or football head; that was its shape. He hid his dinners behind the sofa in the parlor watching "Popeye" or "The Three Stooges." Walking home alone from school, he saw the word: fuck. He asked his Momma, what did it mean, this word, this "foock" he said he saw on the sidewalk printed in chalk. Later he saw the religious plaque the Meyers kids gave him for his birthday: God is love. He asked his Momma, after staring at it for some time, did she know that God is dog backwards?

After Moses took over, Sonny had a cup of coffee with him. Eleven o'clock was slow for a Saturday night. There was a convention in town this weekend, salesmen for cable TV together at the downtown motor hotel. It meant for good business all around: the hookers made out, the pushers found the men in leisure suits and white shoes and imitation gold chains suckers for grass and soppers, and occasionally cocaine. They told them how much the girls liked the stuff, and the johns almost always fell. It made for funny stories at the QuikStar when the salesmen—or the computer wizards or the Elks or the Moose or the Masons—finally cleared out with their tacky clothes and their soiled shoes and their diminished heads, their cocks limp till the next convention, unless in the meantime they got the clap or tried the pot that of course the hookers never smoked: they knew it was laced with angel dust or else was closer to catnip than anything else. They went home to their tract houses and wall-to-wall shag carpet and the dog who shit at least once a week in the workroom or the den or smack in the middle of the kitchen. And they made like angels and practiced speeches on their teenage kids and joined the moral majority and went to church on Sunday like good Americans.

But this was Saturday, and the stories had not begun. Sonny was in no hurry to go home. He lived in Iris Arms, one of those old stone apartment buildings at the edge of downtown that probably was never a good address and now had roaches and red vinyl furniture that had been there for decades, filled with old butt burns, and a slightly greasy, slightly sweaty odor. No one, not even Moses, knew where Sonny lived. His utilities were included in the rent, he had no phone, he owed no debts. His driver's license still bore the old address and he never changed it; he didn't need it, didn't drive any more, didn't have a checking or a savings account. He was paid in cash by the QuikStar manager. He didn't buy much besides food and soda and porn magazines. That was as close as he ever got to touching. And tonight he was in no hurry for his rooms, or for the porn. Tonight he was in one of his rare moods, despite the headache, when he wanted to talk, and Moses was the only person he talked to. He didn't like the 7-3 man. He tried to pretend the QuikStar was like a real job, had ideas about opening his own place soon, stupid guy named Ron Jenkins, pale and skinny and nervous, and a little too bossy. Sonny only talked to Ron about the register ringing up right because he knew Ron dipped, and Sonny wasn't going to get called for it.

Moses was more talkative than usual himself. He leaned back and lit a camel nonfilter, his skinny arms and his bony hands shaking just a little. He'd had three belts of whiskey before he came in; said it quieted the cough. Moses' eyes were watery and the whites kind of yellow. He'd put on a white apron because his grey sweater had a big stain on the front.

"Sonny," he started, "where your Momma at? You ain't mentioned her lately. And when you get that headache you be thinking about her."

"Fuck," Sonny tried to sound tough. "As far as I know she's where she always is, living with my old man. I am thinking about her, because it's been about a month. I'm gonna call her tomorrow, Sunday, when the old man's usually out. He's a bastard, Moses."

"I believe you," Moses answered. "Cause I can see you got a lot of hate in you that ain't right. You too smart for that."

"Smart, fart." Sonny was disgusted. "Lotta good that's ever done me. If it wasn't for my Momma, I'd leave here and go some place warm. I'm hoping the old man croaks first; then I can get me and my Momma a good place to live."

"Well, Sonny, if you waiting for that, you crazy. If your father's mean as you say he is, he ain't never gonna die. Mean ones last forever."

"Well," Sonny heaved a big ragged sigh. He was sweating a little, even in November, from the headache. His black-framed glasses had slid down his nose, and his black wavy hair was damp. Even his green turtleneck sweater was slightly damp in the armpits. "Gimme a donut, Mo, would ya? And remember, forever can change." Sonny looked down into his coffee, dunking the sugar donut into the white porcelain mug and eating it in two bites. "Guess I may as well go home. Less you wanna play some cards."

"No." Moses was not happy with this talk, something funny in Sonny's eyes tonight, or maybe the kid just needed to see some action. That was probably it. Either way, Moses wasn't in the mood for cards, or this conversation. "Guess I'll see you tomorrow at eleven then."

"Yup. Guess you will. Thanks for the warning." And Sonny was up, putting on his brown tweed coat with the fake fur lining and collar. And then his rubbers. Moses still could not believe that Sonny wore rubbers. His mother had not trained him that well.

Italians must be worse. Or something. Sonny plodded out. It was starting to snow in a wet sort of way. Moses watched him through the window, big lumbering kind of guy, just now with his head tucked down to his chest, and his gait kind of off balance. Moses O'Toole felt a little cold spot in his chest, and he couldn't forget it.

two

Rose DeMarco had the blues. It was hot and humid, and it was July 15. Her mother's birthday. She got in her car and drove to the greenhouse and picked up the flowers. Then back in the car. On the way she thought about her brother Sonny for the first time in a while. Four months. Jesus, she thought, I wonder where the fuck he is. She hadn't seen him since the old man threw him out again. The old man never liked Sonny, just because he hadn't been able to be just like him. As though that were something to wish on anybody. All that macho Italian stuff and Sonny just too sweet for it. Right from the start.

Rose had been ten when Sonny was born. She was thirty-seven now, the same age her mother'd been when she had Sonny. Rose was a Girl Scout then, and she'd practiced on Sonny for her childcare badge. She liked Sonny. He was odd, a loner, never seemed to have friends. But he was sweet, there was no other word for it. Like when he sent her candygrams all through nursing school, or when he would make up stories about the two of them working for a big circus. She remembered their scenario: she would be the barber, and Sonny would be the lion tamer who needed a haircut and a shave. He'd come in the bathroom that was their barber shop and ask the price. She'd sing-song, "shave and a haircut, two bits." He'd sit down on the toilet seat, and she'd lather him up and shave him with a razor without the blade. And Sonny would go on and on about the animals and sometimes the side show people, making up stories for hours.

Maybe he would show up today, out of the blue. He'd come last year, though things were a little different then. She hoped he'd be there.

The sky was gray and Rose wished it would rain, break up the humidity. The flowers she bought were wilting already, even though she'd asked for those special water tubes. Hardly mattered, she supposed. She was there.

Assumption Cemetery was one of those huge places that seemed to sprawl on for miles. One part, the part where her mother was buried, was abutted by an expanse of field. It was quiet, and her mother's grave was in a cluster of trees. Josephine DeMarco, nee Martino, the stone read: wife of Dominic, mother of Rose, Lorraine, and Dominic, Jr. July 15, 1917—November 21, 1983. Jesus, Rose thought, almost two years already. Oh, Momma, how I wish you were here.

She took out the flowers, violets, and lily of the valley, and she took out the holy card of St. Lucy, her mother's favorite saint. Rose had gone to the rectory of St. Vincent's and asked Father Michael for a card with St. Lucy. Sometimes, though Rose had not been to church since the funeral, she did pray to St. Lucy, for her mother.

She sat by the tombstone for awhile. Funny, she thought, Momma never did this for her mother. Always said she hated cemeteries. But Rose liked this ritual; it made her feel calm, at peace. She talked to her mother while she was here, just the two of them. Her father never came to the graveyard. And as for Lorraine, she doubted it. The last time she saw Lorraine was at the funeral. She didn't think Sonny would come today.

Rose leaned back on the tombstone, stretching her blue-jeaned legs out in front of her. The granite scratched her back through the thin black cotton tee shirt. She sat there for about an hour, talking to her mother, telling her how she'd split up with her lover. "And you were right, Momma, about Deborah, we couldn't work it out. I should have listened to you. But you'd be proud of my work. No, not at the hospital, my photographs — the fog series. I've had some accepted by a couple of magazines. No, Momma, they don't pay well. (Rose decided not to tell her they didn't pay at all, except maybe a copy or two.) Funny, Rose thought, all those years she worked at what she didn't like so much — all that cooking, the cleaning, the ironing — and she never got any money for it, but she would worry about Rose not making any money doing something she loved. If she could really talk about it with her mother, Rose was sure she would understand. Yes, Momma, I will try to get them to magazines that pay. Don't worry though, my job at the hospital is enough. I'm head nurse now, Momma, on the pediatric floor. You'd be proud. You would. No, I haven't seen Lorraine or Sonny. I'll try to find them. He's fine. Dad is fine. No, he's not remarried. Who'd want him, huh Momma? I guess you got out the only way you could. No, no problems. No, I'm not upset any more about Deborah. You were right, Momma. Are the violets okay? You let me know if you want anything else, okay Momma? I'm going to stay just a few more minutes."

Rose got up to go. She stood and stretched, ran her hand through her short black hair, and bent over to arrange the flowers one more time. As she did, she saw a big footprint around the back of the grave stone. And a new potted plant, a violet, and it was blooming. Sonny. He had remembered, had come to the cemetery. "Well, you see, Momma, he must be fine. He probably just needs to be alone for awhile. You rest Momma, I'll come back soon. I love you Momma."

three

ROSE DIDN'T KNOW where to begin to look for Sonny. On the way home she thought about it, but Sonny never did have any close friends. He had moved out to the suburbs with the family when he was in grammar school. By then, Rose already had her own place. She remembered how her father wouldn't talk to her for a year after that, calling her a *putona** for moving out before she married. She laughed a little at that—she had never married, would never marry. She wondered how her father explained that to himself. Rose hadn't been particularly close to Sonny over the past few years. There was no rift or argument, but as Sonny got older he seemed to let his feelings show less and less. A couple of years ago she had the last real conversation she could remember having with him. They were home, sitting at the kitchen table drinking coffee. Their parents were out, and Sonny was talking about Linda, his girlfriend since high school.

"I loved her Rosie. I thought maybe we could get married. Probably I'll never get married. She left me. Never even said why, just said it had to stop."

Rose remembered that she had felt uncomfortable with the talk. Something about Sonny's despair and his sense of futility made her sad, brought up her own loneliness. She also knew that Sonny was right; he'd probably never get married.

---

*whore

22

Sonny seemed marked as a loner, and Rose saw a resigned desperation on his face.

The cross, she thought. He was born with that tiny cross in the center of his forehead. Their mother would talk about it, saying how Sonny was blessed by it. It had always made Rose worry though; the cross seemed more stigma than scapular.

She could see the cross when she talked to Sonny. His ache was big. It drew his face tight and pale, and in the fluorescent light of the kitchen the tiny grooves of the cross stood out.

Rose had responded with a triviality, had known it when she said it. "You're young Sonny. You'll find somebody to love you."

Sonny looked up at her. For a second his eyes flashed something Rose hadn't seen often in him. It was rage, or a despair so profound it took on the look of rage, his dark eyes intense and direct.

"Love." Sonny looked down again, then up into Rose's eyes. "I wonder if I'll ever feel it." Sonny put his hand on his stomach, rolled his fingers up towards his chest. "I mean Rosie, I don't know if I'll ever *feel* it."

Rose felt awful thinking of that now. Sometimes just thinking of Sonny got her crying. She understood his desperation, his loneliness. Once, when Sonny was about fourteen, she photographed him with their mother outside a restaurant. It was a holiday, Easter, and their father had disappeared, as he usually did on holidays, to be with his girlfriend. Sonny had just begun to understand what his father's absences meant, and Rose had taken the photograph in front of the restaurant where they were going to have dinner with Aunt Anna, her mother's sister. Sonny stood in a sport coat and tie, his pants a little too short, his hair falling on his forehead despite the Brylcream he'd started to use, his arm awkwardly around his mother's shoulders. He was still skinny. His adolescent body was new to him, that was clear in the picture, but it was his eyes Rose remembered. They were filled with woe too old for him, and you could tell looking at the picture that Sonny felt it, but didn't know it past its feeling.

Rose knew she should look for Sonny. She made up her mind to do it soon, but just now she felt too vulnerable. Breaking up with Deborah had been hard. She had loved Deborah with a passion she didn't know she had. She'd wanted to be possessed, to possess, and in the years she and Deborah had been together — until Deborah's alcoholism became a bigger and bigger part of the relationship, until all there was were fights and silences that alternated — Rose had wanted little more than that passion. The love making that still made it hard for them to totally separate, even their fighting had an edge to it that Rose had to admit she craved. But finally it took its toll, and after the last blowup, Rose hadn't been able to eat or sleep or function at all. She'd had to call in sick to the floor for a week, and when Deborah finally came around again, Rose was too spent to begin with the same intensity. She had been more or less alone for a couple of months now, sleeping better and having fewer bad dreams. Rose was especially pleased with the fog photographs, a series of pictures she'd been working on for almost two years. Recently she'd gone up to Lake Ontario, and in the very early morning she took what she thought might be the best of the lot — maybe even the conclusion to the sequence — the heavy, gray mist burning off, the fog just lifting to reveal a strip of incredible blue, just a sliver of it, shaped like an almond, or an eye slowly opening. Rose was planning to mat them her next day off from Peds, and then get ready for a group show at the Women's Center.

To look for Sonny just now would bring too much unhappiness back again. Sonny's loneliness and sorrow took a different form from her own. Rose had learned long ago how to survive, but Sonny was burdened by his illnesses, and now by his weight, and most of all by his sensitivity. Rose had found ways to get that sensitivity to work for her—taking care of kids was one way, and her pictures another. She knew that was not just because she had a brain, but because she looked right and had a fast mouth. Her mother used to tell her that her tongue was her worst enemy: she could never stay silent like her mother did when her father yelled. Rose always talked back, no matter how many beatings she got with the belt, no matter how many times she ignored her mother's biting her lower lip—a signal to Rose to shut up.

To find Sonny, Rose knew, was to decide to try and help him somehow, and at the moment she wasn't up to it. But she had promised her mother to look for him. If the plant hadn't been there today, she would have tried right away. But the plant had been there, and Rose thought she could wait a little longer. She would go and see her father soon, see if he'd softened up any, and if he had, maybe then she could start to look for her brother.

four

WHEN MOSES O'TOOLE checked out to that asshole Ron Jenkins, he had smoked two packs of camels and drunk a lot of bad coffee. He couldn't get Sonny off his mind, not that there was a whole lot else he could think about. Wished he could call *his* Momma, even if it was once a month on Sunday, but she was dead. Dead a long time now. When he was twenty and she was just thirty-six she died in a city hospital with her appendix busted. Died right out there in the waiting room while somebody else, somebody white was saved. Till Sonny, he never liked to talk to white people after that.

Take Ron: he was pretty typical — smart-assed, talking down, always making sure to add all the "ings" to his words in the fuckin QuikStar. Moses also knew that every now and then Ron dipped his fishy white hand in the register for a reason. Slimy old Ron had a favorite hooker, name of Lucinda Potts, big chesty girl with violet perfume and Dixie Peached hair, a dark brown complexion and a high attitude when she was workin, and especially when Ron was around. Moses and Lucinda dished Ron plenty when he wasn't around, or sometimes they did it right in front of him. He was such a diddly-ass thing, never could tell the difference.

But Sonny was just himself. Miserable, overweight, not too clean or neat, but he didn't make no bones or attitudes up. Sonny was just a kid, Moses knew, even though he knew Sonny wanted to act like he been around. Moses figured Sonny kept his world so small on purpose, cause Sonny was smart enough to know nobody gonna like him how he kept himself, and he seemed to wanna keep himself the way he was. And so, Moses figured, in his own way Sonny was safe. But the kid seemed awful miserable. He wanted to call it sad but he couldn't because even if it sure wasn't happy, it wasn't sad so much as it was miserable, kind of mean-like sometimes, or sort of like Sonny was taking some bad pleasure in his raggedy life. Moses was so juiced from the coffee he kept thinking on Sonny till he got home.

The Clinton Hotel on Jefferson Street was filled with people like Moses, mostly men, but there were a couple of old ladies who had been there for years. Moses had a suite. They still called it that at the Clinton Hotel. What that meant was that he had his one room, but there was a hot plate and a sink and the cupboard the hot plate stood on. They called that a kitchenette. And he was real close to the bathroom, which was convenient. Aside from those luxuries, his room was like all the other sixty rooms: painted a pale sickening green, with some kind of gray linoleum with speckles in it, and one light that had a shattered fixture, like someone had taken a bat to it. Moses never bothered to fix it. Long as he could change the bulb without cutting his hand, it didn't matter to him. He had an old torn up couch and a little radio that worked on batteries, a carton of camels and a half pint of whiskey, and a little table over near the kitchenette where he liked to listen to the radio and read the paper. He had one other thing, a picture of his Momma, and he kept it tacked on to the green wall right over his table.

Moses looked at the photo when he got home. He thought if he could talk to her he'd only tell her the good things, like how he finally got a steady job, and like that they got all of it when he had his operation. So that she could believe things were a little different anyway now. He'd tell her about Sonny too, cause he was worried some on Sonny, and maybe his Momma might tell him something. Not that he'd ever listened to her when she was alive, but he'd learned a little since then.

Moses sat at his table thinking on Sonny and reading the paper and talking a little to his Momma. He had two shots of whiskey to get him tired, and he laid down on the couch to catch some sleep. The last thing he thought about as he fell asleep was that funny cold spot he'd felt in his chest when Sonny walked out in the snow.

five

ON SUNDAY SONNY SLEPT till noon. He dreamed through his headache. The dreams were always in color when he had the headache.

In the dream he saw his Sicilian grandmother, the one they told him was a witch. She told him to come with her and she would teach him what he wanted to know. She spoke Sicilian, which he didn't know, but he understood her perfectly. She had his father's face, only thinner, and while Dominic was almost bald, she had thick black hair and a widow's peak. She told Sonny she knew magic, but he knew she wanted him to die. That's why she beckoned him to go with her. In the dream he pulled out a long skinny knife that had just been sharpened. He spoke only once in the dream, and that was to say, "I'll kill you first even if you are dead, even if you want me dead. Because you deserve a death. Capice?"*

When he woke up his headache was gone, and there was a gray light coming in through the window in the living room. He'd fallen asleep on the couch and had rolled over onto the bag of potato chips. Everything was crumbs. He woke saying oh fuck, but in a good-hearted kind of way. He did not recall the dream. He got up and put some water on to boil and without washing his face or brushing his teeth, he went down to the 7-Eleven on the corner to get the *Herald American*. He

---

*understand

29

came back and made a cup of instant coffee and lay back down on the couch and read the paper until it was time to go to work. He wanted to leave a little earlier today because he had to call his Momma around two when the old man was most likely to be out.

◆

At two o'clock Sonny heaved himself up off the couch. He peered at his big face in the foggy bathroom mirror: two days growth of beard, thick and black and mean looking. Even he would call it that. Face getting flabbier by the minute; he didn't care. He took his glasses off and rubbed the red grooves on his crooked nose. Oh what the fuck, he thought, may as well shave if I'm gonna call Momma.

He lathered up with the Old Spice and tried to coax some good hot water from the tap. It was lukewarm, the blade was well used, and the shave was not so much a shave as a pulling away of the biggest of his whiskers. What's the difference anyway, he thought, she can't see over the phone and nobody in the Star's gonna care. He wished his Momma lived right here. The place would be okay if it was cleaned up. He finished, half-heartedly rinsed the blade, put on a cleaner sweater, and grabbing some change from the mayonnaise jar on the bathroom shelf, went to make his call.

He remembers his Momma making him food special because he hated meatballs on Sunday. She even used to let him have TV dinners. He remembers when she realized he was dumping them behind the sofa. She was hurt then because she'd only got them for him. He couldn't help it; it all tasted funny. He just wanted to watch "Popeye" and "The Three Stooges" and not have to think about anything else, especially not when his father came home after everyone had eaten because he came home so late then. Late and crabby and mean.

*Like nobody could talk then or especially laugh. Because
then his father might go crazy. Like that Christmas when his
sisters liked their dolls but only said "thanks <u>Mom</u>." And his
father left on Christmas even though his Momma cried and
his sisters cried. Sonny remembers this Christmas as he goes
to call his mother. In two weeks it will be Thanksgiving.*

At two-fifteen he put his money in the phone booth and
dialed. The phone rang and rang on the other end: he
counted ten times. She's not there. Oh fuck, he thought, why
not? The old man probably dragged her out to his Uncle
Tony's. I bet he still does that even though he knows she
doesn't like Uncle Tony *or* Aunt Mary. Fuck, she's been
home every other Sunday. She said she'd make sure to stay
home Sundays till he called again. He dialed again, just to
make sure. Fifteen times, fuck it, answer.

Sonny's palms were sweating in the booth even though it
was thirty degrees and beginning that wet snow again. What
am I gonna do if I don't get her? His head ached. At two-
thirty he tried once more: twenty rings, no answer. He came
out of the booth, his face white and strained, put the change
back in his pocket, and headed for work.

"You're early Sonny." Ron's voice disgusted him. Like as
though Sonny didn't know that himself.

"What of it?" Sonny was belligerent. When Ron didn't
answer, Sonny said it again. "What of it?"

"Nothing of it. That's what. Unless you want there to be."
Slimy Ron was like that; always turning around an argument
so you looked responsible.

"Why don't I check you out Ron*ie*?" Sonny loved to make
the Ron*ie* like that so that old slimy Ron was sissified.
"Cause Lucinda's just around the corner. She asked me to tell
you."

Ron was such a jerk that he believed it. Sonny just wanted
Ron out of there so he could have a cup of coffee and think

about what to do. They checked out, and Ron's register was on for once. Sonny wondered for a minute how Ron was doing it cause he knew he was still dipping. Fuck it, he thought. More power to him.

When Ron was gone, it was quiet. There was only one customer, an old wino named George who dozed in a booth while his coffee went cold. Sonny was nervous. What if something had happened to her? What if Moses was right about the mean ones outlasting everyone else? He leaned forward onto the counter and tried to think. He had to slice tomatoes for the special, like anybody really thought it was special. Meatloaf, instant mashed potatoes, canned peas, and a slice of fresh tomato. He couldn't believe that fresh tomato. He hated it too because it hurt his fingers around where he bit his nails when the juice of the tomatoes got in. Sonny went into the cooler and got them, came back, wiped off the cutting board, and reached for the knife. The blade glinted for a moment under the lights, and for a second Sonny remembered a line from his forgotten dream: *"I'll kill you first even if you are dead, even if you want me dead."* Weird, he thought, where'd that come from. He sliced the tomatoes slowly, letting go of the phrase he'd momentarily remembered. He decided he'd just have to wait until next Sunday to call her again, unless he tried to call during the week and risk catching his father at home. The bastard, Sonny thought, big shot with his roll of bills and his sleazy friends. He liked to think of himself as retired now, growing vegetables in the backyard, listening to opera records, pushing Sonny's Momma around. And she stayed stuck with him, would never think of leaving, stuck forever. Fuck, thought Sonny, forever can change.

It was a slow night; Sonny only had to make up eight orders of the special. The regulars started coming in around ten when the last of the conventioneers left town. Moses came in at eleven, but the place was pretty well crowded and Sonny had no chance to talk to him. Moses was quiet anyway, didn't even remember to ask Sonny if his call had gone through. Sonny had thought for sure Moses would ask him. His head was pounding again, and he was crabby and out of sorts. He was back in his own place by eleven-thirty, with a warm rag thrown over his eyes. He thought maybe that would help. Monday was his day off.

six

HE WAS IN THE *playground at St. Vincent's, in the third grade. It was early November, and it was beginning to rain — that fine cold rain warning of winter. He was in the playground, and it was recess. Sister Fabia stood beneath the sheltered stairway that led into the auditorium. The boys were playing dodge ball, and he wanted to play. Two big boys were made captains. They chose sides, but no one chose him. Sister Fabia said then he should be in the middle and whichever team hit him with the ball would get him on their team. He wouldn't do that. He said, "No, Sister, I can't play." He knew he was going to cry. He said, "I don't feel good, Sister. I'll just watch." He walked over to the side of the playground, well outside the circle playing dodge ball, far away from Sister Fabia who stood in the protected doorway with her hands tucked under the bib of her habit fingering the large wooden rosary beads she wore around her waist beneath the habit.*

Sonny stood there with his scrawny shoulders hunched a little forward. His blue tie poked out from the yellow slicker he wore, hood up, his head covered. His glasses kept fogging up from the rain, but he was glad it was raining so he could cry a little. He didn't know what it was he felt. He only knew it as an awful loneliness from deep inside, a loneliness separate from the want for friends or company, a loneliness that only the different know: how it feels to be invisible, apart. Sonny's chest felt funny. He thought of his Momma's canary, Tweetie, its soft body. He had felt it through the metal bars of Tweetie's little cage where it stood by the window in the kitchen, had stood with his finger marveling at its softness. He knew it would be easy to hurt Tweetie, so he was always careful to go easy on it. He stood in the fine rain shivering a little and thinking of the canary until the bell rang and they filed back inside for catechism.

seven

WHEN SONNY WOKE on Monday, it was too early, six-thirty. The sky was just beginning to open. He lay on his back with his glasses off, and he wondered what he should do. It was very quiet. It was raining.

Once, just before Thanksgiving, Rose took him downtown to watch the Thanksgiving parade. It had been raining, and they went on the bus to downtown. Sonny was four or five. Rose had a little red change purse with two dollars in it. She told him it was enough for the bus and for hot chocolate and toasted corn muffins at Woolworth's after. Before they went on the bus they played circus. Rose shaved Sonny and combed his hair, taking great pains with the part. Sonny felt important going with Rose. She even put his father's after-shave on his cheeks after the shave, and she let him give the bus driver the money. They stood in the light rain and watched the parade go by. He liked the Mickey Mouse float the best next to Santa Claus at the end, with his reindeer. And Rose surprised him with an extra quarter for a red balloon with Santa Claus' face on it. When they went to Woolworth's to warm up with the hot chocolate and the warm corn muffins, Sonny held tight to his balloon. He liked the way it looked at the counter, with all the kids holding balloons and the waitresses even smiling and hurrying up.

Sonny lay in bed thinking. It was getting close to Thanksgiving, and he had never been alone on that holiday before.

Last year he had seen Rose. He wondered if he could call her, try to see her. But then Sonny remembered Deborah. He couldn't understand how Rose could be with Deborah. When she told him she was gay a couple of years earlier, he told her: "Everything else in this family goes on the back burner. This is the worst." Later he told her he guessed it was okay, she seemed happy. Still, he couldn't understand it. He had a feeling that maybe Rose wouldn't like him as much any more. But he missed Rose, missed talking to her. He thought maybe he should get up, run down to the QuikStar, catch Moses going off, maybe have coffee with him someplace else so they wouldn't have to pay any mind to Ron. Sonny couldn't decide what to do. He lay there thinking until he fell back to sleep.

He was about nine, coming home from church with Rose. It was summer. When they turned the corner they could smell their Momma's sauce cooking. Then they stopped walking because they saw their Momma in an old car, a red Packard, and she was in the driver's seat. There was no steering wheel. The car was crowded with people. Sonny and Rose didn't know them. Their Momma said, "I'm going, don't try to find me. I'll get in touch with you when it's time." Rose and Sonny both started to cry, then scream. Sonny wanted to race after her, but his feet wouldn't move.

He woke with his face wet with tears, a huge sob stuck in his throat. "Oh God" was all he managed to say before he let the sob that caught him off guard come out. He couldn't stop crying, he heard the rain on the window. It was eleven-thirty. He had to try to see his Momma. After awhile he got up, threw on some clothes, and ran down to the 7-Eleven store. He bought some new blades and the morning paper. An hour later he was on his way: freshly shaven for a change, a clean shirt under his tweed coat. He left the smell of aftershave and a steamy mirror behind.

eight

SONNY WAITED OUTSIDE of Dey's for the bus to North Syracuse. He had to try to see his mother. He thought if he could get the bus and get out there, he could figure a way to get to his parents' house. If he was careful, maybe he could see her through a window, or maybe she would come out just as he arrived. He waited until four to get the bus, counting on the early winter darkness to help him.

Sonny wandered about, lost in the early Christmas shoppers and the downtown business people. He spent some time in one of those game rooms, playing Asteroids and Space Invaders for about an hour. He liked the computer games because he could play them alone, because the beeping sound that came with the game took him far away. He had hot chocolate at Woolworth's just before he went back out into the rain to wait for the bus.

"Hey, Sonny, whatcha up to?" Sonny turned, surprised at hearing his name. It was Lucinda Potts, and she had her baby Dawn with her. Dawn was wrapped up in one of those flowered baby buntings, safe from the rain. Lucinda balanced Dawn, a big purse covered with little mirrors, and an umbrella. She was out of her working clothes. Lucinda was another person when she was off. Her high attitude was just a facade for the johns and the QuikStar.

In her own life, she was a friendly, even warm woman. She was twenty-two, lived by herself with her baby, tried to get by as best she could. Lucinda liked Sonny. Lots of nights when she had been flat broke, especially right after Dawn was born and she couldn't work, Sonny gave her a cheeseburger and fries, and a large milk to go for the baby, and never rang it up. Though Lucinda hooked with Ron, she wouldn't think of asking him for help. Sonny was different. She never even had to ask Sonny. He just knew, because one night she'd come in around nine with Dawn, ordered coffee, and Sonny must have seen the look on her face when the guy next to her got the special. The beef stew looked warm and smelled good, and Lucinda hadn't eaten since the night before. Sonny never said nothing, just cooked up a cheeseburger and fries and said, "I'll put it on your bill, Lucinda." Said it like the Star was really a place let you run up a bill. Lucinda had eaten it all and took the milk with her to feed to Dawn later on. When she got ahead on money, she tried to pay Sonny, and he'd said, "Oh forget it. They'll never miss it and you would."

Today Lucinda wore faded blue jeans, the bottoms muddy from dragging in the rain. Her navy blue peacoat was wide open, the buttons gone. "Watcha up to?" she said again.

"I'm waiting for a bus," was all Sonny said, at first.

"Hmph, like I can't see that. A bus to where?"

"To the shopping center in North Syracuse. Christmas shopping. Why you want to know?"

"Cause that's just where I'm going," Lucinda grinned at Sonny. "And if *you* be going there too, then we can go together, Cause maybe I need some help with Dawn. Dja ever hold a baby?"

Sonny had been getting pissed till she mentioned the baby. Then he thought he could go with Lucinda and Dawn. Sure, what difference did it make really? After they shopped, maybe Lucinda would let him buy her a cup of coffee or something. He could still go out to the house after that. He hadn't held a baby in a long time.

Lorraine had been eighteen when she had the baby. Her name was Donna. He only saw her a couple of times. Once, Lorraine put a big pillow on his knees and said, "Okay, Sonny, you can hold her." He was ten. He held the baby, this new Donna, on his knees, on the pillow. He touched her face with his finger; it was so soft. He touched her head, the fine light brown hair. Lorraine told him to watch the soft spot. She showed him where it was, right in the center of her tiny little head that was round as an orange, and it had a soft spot. If Sonny kept his finger on that soft spot, he could feel a beat. Donna's heart beat, Rose told him.

"Sure I held a baby. A long time ago, but I held a baby. But I don't have all day Lucinda, just a couple of hours."

"That be fine. I gotta work y'know Sonny. I don't get days off like you do. Here's the bus."

They got on the bus, and when they sat down, Lucinda turned to Sonny. "Y'wanna hold her now, Sonny? Give me a break so I can have a cigarette."

Sonny took Dawn. She was only five months old. Sonny pulled the bunting away so he could see her face. She was dark brown, same as Lucinda, but her hair was like a thick carpet of shiny black curls. She held her hand in a tiny fist curled up to her mouth. Sonny touched her hand; and Dawn opened up her eyes and looked at Sonny and grinned, at the same time grabbing Sonny's finger in her little fist. They sat like that on the bus, the three of them silent: Lucinda smoking and looking out the window, Sonny holding the baby, Dawn herself just smiling or sleeping all the way. Sonny felt good for the first time in awhile.

nine

Sonny never did get out to his Momma's house. When they finished shopping, Sonny and Lucinda were both hungry, and Lucinda let him buy dinner at a Chinese restaurant in the mall. Dawn was being awfully good. Sonny was feeling close to happy. He'd even gotten in the mood to shop: he bought Moses a small leather-covered flask, small enough to keep in his pocket; he bought his Momma some perfume, Blue Grass, her favorite; and he saw something that he thought Rose would like—a red plaid, woolen scarf. And when Lucinda was looking for a sweater for Dawn, Sonny saw a small stuffed dog, tan with floppy ears and sad eyes, and on impulse he bought it for Dawn. Lucinda laughed and said, "Now what Dawn gonna give you Sonny?" Sonny said, "She's just gonna let me hold her again."

By the time they were through eating it was about seven-thirty, and Lucinda started being in a hurry to get back. Sonny just couldn't let her try to go back by herself because now she had all her packages to carry as well as the baby, the umbrella, and the purse. Dawn was starting to get fussy, crying a little and sneezing some. Lucinda took a pink hat from her purse and put it on Dawn. "Maybe she be catchin a cold. The girl who watch her nights got a bad one." The pink woolen hat matched Dawn's tiny sweater. All the way back into the

41

city Sonny held Dawn on his lap, sometimes bringing her up
to hug against his chest, and Lucinda dozed.

They got off where they started, in front of Dey's. Now Lucinda had to get over to West Colvin where she lived. Sonny,
flushed by the day, got them a cab. "Maybe I'll see you tomorrow at the Star, Sonny. Thanks a lot." Lucinda and Dawn
were gone. Sonny was alone again with his three packages, and
his chest feeling warm where Dawn had lain against it.

ten

SONNY WOKE UP with a headache. It had started during the night. He got up once from it, took three extra strength aspirin, and went back to sleep.

He was at a family party, some celebration, or some holiday. He stood in the parlor of the old house talking to his cousins Sammy and Eddie. Another cousin, Jimmy, the retarded one, sat on the blue mohair sofa, drooling and playing with an empty tin can. Then his mother came out of the kitchen. She came up to him, her face confused, her eyes vacant, staring just past him. "Where's the white bird?" she said. "I can't find the white bird. You know where it is, Sonny. Where is it, where's the white bird?" In the dream he could feel the urgency. He could almost see the white bird with its very soft body, but he didn't know what she was talking about. Jimmy started to wail. Sonny stood and looked at his mother. She kept staring off just past him, just kept repeating, "Where's the white bird, Sonny? Where's the white bird?"

Sonny woke in a panic, screaming, "I don't know Momma, I don't know!" But even as he woke he thought he did know; he just couldn't place it. He could see the white bird, sort of like a pigeon, like outside of city hall where he and his Momma used to catch the bus back home after they went down-town. He was afraid. He thought the white bird meant death. He didn't know why, but he was sure that was the message. His chest felt funny, sort of sick or shaky. His heart was pounding.

eleven

THOUGH IN FACT Sonny worked and lived not far from where Rose nursed at the medical center, their worlds were so different that the likelihood of their running into one another was slim. The medical center was in the university section; the QuikStar was in the heart of downtown. Rose hadn't shopped downtown in years; and Sonny, knowing Rose worked in the university area, made sure to stay away from it. In the months since the visit to her mother's grave, Rose had thought often about trying to find Sonny. She really had no idea where to begin, though. She just assumed he was still in the city because she couldn't imagine where else Sonny would go. He'd never been away from his home town, so it wasn't like he could have just gone off somewhere. No, Rose thought, Sonny was most likely living somewhere in Syracuse.

Now, a couple of weeks before the two-year anniversary of her mother's death, Rose thought again about looking for Sonny. She considered trying to get a hold of Lorraine. That would be hard but not impossible. On second thought, she doubted it would be helpful. Lorraine lived on the west side the last Rose knew. God knows how she was supporting herself and Donna, or whether she still hung out with junkies.

◆

Lorraine DeMarco Fuller had been off drugs for four years. She was settled into a trailer out to Elbridge with a man named Curtis Fuller, a Black man she met in a neighborhood grocery store. Lorraine was now a kind of super housewife: she clipped coupons and saved cartons and labels and sent them in for refunds. She'd learned to drive and had another baby, Curtis Jr., and they called him just Junior. Junior was almost two, and Donna was a senior in high school.

Lorraine thought about Rose and Sonny, especially about Sonny, because she'd always felt something about Sonny made him need protection. Rose—she didn't know. She thought Rose kind of had attitudes. Actually, she wasn't sure if Rose had ever really liked her. Lorraine had had it hard enough: there was Rose, two years older, *prettier* is what everybody always said, one of those goody two-shoes in high school, passing everything and running for student council. Rose liked penny loafers and matching skirts and sweaters; Lorraine had wanted a black leather jacket more than anything and had finally gotten one. She had to laugh at that: she in leather, Rose with her rah friends. She remembered, though, how much Rose had loved the leather jacket, and Lorraine knew it was because she looked tough.

As she got older and settled down some, Lorraine understood it a little more. It had been awful for all of them, but Rosie was supposed to be able to handle it. Rosie never cried, as far as Lorraine could remember, always tried to keep the old man under control. Lorraine remembered the night they brought her home, the night before she left. She could still see Rosie's face, the horror on it when she looked at Lorraine. But she also remembered Rosie helping her into the bathtub after the beating she got. Then when Rosie came out, Lorraine had to laugh. Christ, she thought, the three of us: a dyke, a junkie, and a weirdo. Well whaddya want the way things were?

◆

Time, like an elephant, had crowded them all. The sweep of it nudging past the simplicity of reason, reason an unaffordable expense, so that all was passion in a pure state — every argument, every whim or task or regret, every kiss at night or the neglected kiss at night. Mornings the coffee woke Rosie, while Lorraine slept on, and she learned to recognize the air of her mother's time, skimmed off the top of day like a luxury, its breath palpable and urgent. This Rosie carried with her always, a kind of time that moved in her, the memory that was now as well as then; the urgency and passion of a life that is simply necessary on its own terms, like it or not. It was a vision that turned inward, that played a sort of interior movie: the camera angled on the light, the slant or shift of it, how it knew that light, yielding up some sharp-edged thing or something worn on the edges, the glint of sex, or the grieving tear the second before it drops. And the confusion, the constant misfocusing, the question, the *why* that played in all of their minds shunted off to a side of the picture, never looked at clearly for the terror of rage, or the rage of terror, never understood, just simply or harshly filled with a burning need for motion, just lived in its own ache to live, to keep breathing.

◆

When she met Curtis, Lorraine figured she had waited long enough. She was tired, she was thirty-two, and Donna was beginning to be a brat, wanting fancy haircuts and talking about boys. She'd been off heroin for four years now, though she knew Rose and the old man and probably even Sonny thought she was still messed up. She didn't get straight for any good reason, had never been picked up except the time when she was a kid and they brought her home. She'd managed as best she could, finding guys to cop for her when she was out of work.

When she stopped it was because some wise-mouth guy who figured her for easy lays for him and his buddies told her she'd never stop using stuff and that she was getting old. He told her she was like a dozen other chicks he knew, strung out for years, and how maybe in a couple of years it could be Donna'd be the trade. Lorraine was not a sentimental mother. It wasn't so much that this creep threatened her. Even though she knew that wouldn't happen to Donna if she could help it, what pissed her off was him trying to tell her he knew her, knew the mold she came out of. It was like the first time she stopped, the early time, just after she left home. She'd gone to a drop-in center, and the dude there told her he knew her, too; told her she'd never stop unless she checked into a program. One thing Lorraine always hated was going public, or doing things in crowds, and as soon as that counselor started talking about group therapy and having to stay overnight in some shelter, Lorraine bolted. The guy told her she'd be back, back like the rest of them: back sick and broke and probably crawling with lice and VD and no hope.

So Lorraine had stopped. She found her friend from high school who'd been through it herself. She holed up with Margie Laski for a couple of months; came back out of it slow, but came back out; got a job on the line at Magnavox, and stayed there and stayed straight until a year after Donna was born. She stayed straight until after she'd gone back home with the baby once or twice and saw the way the old man treated her, and how Rosie was kind of ashamed about the whole thing, and how her Momma had wanted to take

Donna cause she was afraid Lorraine was still on drugs, still hooking for money.

Only Sonny had been clean of heart, too young to understand all that was on everybody else's mind — Sonny touching Donna with his skinny little finger, touching her soft spot like it was made out of gold. Lorraine remembered that because there was such a gentleness in Sonny when he held Donna that Lorraine thought her heart would break. When she left, she wished she could have taken Sonny with her: She wished she had it in her to save him from what she knew was inevitable, because even then the old man was ridiculing Sonny for being skinny or afraid of things, calling him a sissy and a crybaby when all Sonny was was soft on the inside and filled up with a lotta love that couldn't come out right except with Momma.

Lorraine went back to drugs the same way she came off them: not for a good reason; just because that was what there was to do. Funny thing was, even now — even straight and living with Curtis and happy enough clipping coupons and cleaning the trailer, taking care of Junior, and helping Donna get ready for dates and listening to Donna's friends' problems because their own mothers didn't want to hear them — Lorraine knew she'd do it all the same again. She couldn't see how it could have ever been different, things being what they were, and she figured even if she'd fucked up some, she'd done it all by herself.

That was a real DeMarco trait, and they all found their own ways of working it out. Fucked up or not, they had pride.

twelve

HE NEVER STOPPED reaching across the bed for Josie. Two years after her death, two years of sleeping alone night after night, he woke in the middle of foggy dreams, or at the light of sunrise, and reached for her. Over the years Dominic had been, in his own way, faithful to his wife. He'd been to bed with other women but always returned home before daylight, always began the day with Josie. He had to admit that after her death the thought that he could now spend the night, all night, with whomever he chose had crossed his mind. But he couldn't.

He had tried to a couple of times, but always, just before falling asleep, he would see Josie. He could see her small and delicate frame sleeping curled slightly in a pale blue nightgown, her hand tucked just under her chin as though she had fallen asleep wondering, her hair mussed and wispy on the pillow. Dominic, when he had these flashes of Josephine, saw them from changing times during their forty-year marriage. Josie on their wedding night honeymooning in New York City, wearing a white silky nightgown, her black hair thick and long and loose against his chest. He remembered her being both timid and bold at once. Josie, when he first saw her months after Rosie was born, falling asleep with the baby held against her breast. Josie getting up at 3:00 a.m. when he'd walk in, fixing him eggs in the middle of the night. Josie, sleepy and complacent, giving him her quiet company despite his wanderings.

Dominic would see his Josie, and a small and tender and decisive tug would win in his chest. It was love. He never felt guilt making him move. If in fact it had been guilt, he probably would have stayed; for he was an impulsive and passionate man who followed always what he knew was true for him, despite the consequences. Always at night what he felt was the tenderest love for Josie, and he longed for the feel of her familiar body next to him. So he had kept his habit, even after her death, of returning to their bed with its blue satin bedspread, to their room, their wedding photographs, and Josie's scented presence. When the kids had come to take her clothes and belongings, Dominic had made them leave the Blue Grass perfume, a couple of her nightgowns, and their photographs. In this way he kept her close to him.

Dominic knew he had not made life easy for Josie and that she stuck by him despite it. The early years of their marriage, before he left for the war, had been tense. There was never enough money, and even then he was running around with other women. They lived with his mother, Filomena, a strong-willed, iron-fisted matriarch, whom Dominic adored. Filomena took to Josephine the way she did to all who were not members of her immediate family: she was intimidating and aloof, and she made Josie more timid than she already was by nature. If she occasionally allowed Josie to cook, she always criticized the results. She never stopped letting Josephine know that it was she, Filomena, who best understood Dominic. Josie did not thrive there, but when she brought it up with Dominic, he would fly into a rage. If she hated his mother, he would say, that was her problem. He was staying. They didn't have enough money for their own place, and no, of course Josie could not work so they could have enough money.

Dominic knew that Josie was right, knew they should move to their own place, but nothing in him was prepared to defy his mother and leave. She was a saint to him. She had raised seven kids as good as alone. His father, Pasquale, had been a rough and lazy man who worked occasionally and used Filomena to vent his outrage and lust. Nothing more. By the time Dominic was in grammar school, Pasquale was almost always drunk and hostile. When he died, Dominic, at seventeen, was relieved. He was the baby of the family, and only one sister, Theresa, was at home. Until he married Josie, his life had been calm and well cared for by his mother and sister. When Josie came into the household, Theresa was married and living with her husband. There sprang up between the two women in his life a tension and competition he was unready for. His solution was to throw up his hands and turn it into a fight with Josie: she had no respect, he'd say. What would she do if her mother were still alive? There was simply no way that Dominic could willfully leave his mother's house.

This situation might have gone on and on, but in November of 1942 Dominic enlisted in the army, the one sure way he could leave his mother's house and the situation within it without having to choose between his mother and his wife. Josie, of course, had to stay there with Filomena. Had it not been for Dominic's finally allowing her to get a job at the telephone company—after all, it was wartime—Josie would have suffered even more. The problem of moving into their own place was solved for the moment. Dominic didn't know if he'd come back at all by the time the whole thing was over.

He returned a few times on leaves, twice in close succession, and the second of these two visits was to be the last before he was shipped overseas. It was December 1943, and it was the time of two events that would change things forever for Dominic and Josie. On their fourth wedding anniversary, December 12, Josie told Dominic she was pregnant; the baby was due in August. Dominic felt a motion around his heart, as though a sparrow were fluttering its wings. It was one of his first sensations of tenderness, and it was directed toward both Josie and their baby, and even toward himself for his part in this. Josie was proud and nervous, her olive skin flushed slightly with the news. Dominic had stared at her, finding it hard to believe that his little Josie, looking skinny and delicate to him just then, was pregnant, and finding it harder to believe that he would almost certainly not be able to be home when the baby was born.

He shipped out just after Christmas and was sent first to France and later to India. He was there when the second event took place: on March 14, 1944, Filomena died suddenly. Dominic would always remember that he could not be at two of the most important occurrences in his life. He blamed the army for this, and felt, afterwards, that the army owed him something for it. In August of that same year, Dominic's and Josephine's first child was born, and he was still in India flying surveillance missions. He did not learn of Rosie's birth till nearly a month after it happened. The news came in a letter from Josie with a picture of the baby. She was a tiny thing with a lot of black hair combed up like a rooster's and with Josie's large dark eyes looking up at him. Josie had written across the photo: "To Daddy, from your daughter Rosie. Hurry home, I love you."

But he did not get home until just after VJ Day, in October 1945. Rose was fourteen months old, and Dominic was filled with hope and excitement about his life.

That excitement was soon to include a touch of bitterness, a resentment, small at first but growing. Before the war, Dominic had been used to having two women cater to him, and now Josie, in charge of the big house Dominic and his family had grown up in, and a devoted mother to Rosie, did not always have the time to baby her husband. Dominic saw this as neglect, as Josie not being as good a wife and mother as his mother had been. He took to throwing this up to her whenever they argued, a fact that brought out the stubbornness in Josie. Powerless in the world beyond her home, and steeped in the role she knew as well as breathing, being the good Italian wife — docile and attentive, mostly silent, understanding and forgiving — she found the one way to rebel against Dominic's tirades. Often she forgot to strain the sauce, knowing the seeds drove him crazy; or she'd iron everything except his handkerchiefs; or she mismatched socks. If she really wanted to get to him, she would leave the bathroom uncleaned for days on end, watching the mold creep up between and around the tiles, insidious, commiserating.

But she was also there, tender and vulnerable to him. That she loved him deeply was clear, even in the passion of their arguments. To Dominic she was the one innocent thing that was only his. Even Rose, he knew, would eventually grow away from them. But Josie was his light. She understood what no one remotely guessed about Dominic DeMarco: his vulnerability, his alarm in and at the world, his defensiveness about being Italian. This from years of being tormented and teased by calls of *greaseball* or *guinea,* accused of being dirty or lazy, and from an acute memory of the time he'd been fired from a job as a stock boy, long before the war. He was sixteen, working at the five and dime — twelve, fourteen, sometimes sixteen hours a day. He worked hard and was honest. After three months he had asked about a promotion, and the manager fired him on the spot, telling him, "You're a *wop* DeMarco, don't forget it." He hadn't.

To the rest of the world, Dominic DeMarco was a tough guy, a guy who would do anything for you unless you crossed him, a guy who always had his suits tailor-made and flashed

money when he had it—or he wasn't around—a guy with a
very short fuse and a tendency to fist fight. He worked construction for awhile, booked numbers and horses for years,
quit construction to book full time, and quit that a few years
after the kids were all out of high school. He had run a small
trucking firm ever since with two of his brothers, called ADS
Trucking Co., for Anthony, Dominic, and Salvatore. Dominic was pleased with their outfit; for even though he was in
his forties when the company was formed, it showed him that
Tony and Sal finally accepted him. As the baby of the family,
and as his mother's pet, he had always been seen as the kid, in
need of protection. Perhaps to change this image, Dominic
had taken to fighting as a boy, a taste he never abandoned,
and to mouthing off to anyone who came close to rubbing
him the wrong way. He was raised to believe that the only
way to get respect in the world was to wield power, to be
tough *and* smooth. He watched his brothers, practiced, and
learned well.

In 1946 Lorraine was born. Josie had been initially upset
with the pregnancy. She wanted time, a little time for herself
before having another baby, and the months of carrying Lorraine were difficult for her. She didn't feel well. Rose was two
and into everything, and Dominic was rarely around. But
along Lorraine had come, a baby as unlike her sister as was
possible. Rose had slept through the night almost from the
start; Lorraine was colicky and awoke several times during
the night until she was nearly a year old. And then she
became a solitary little girl—reticent, easygoing to a fault.
Rose was independent, talked constantly, and as she got older
was always in fights, often to protect her kid sister. If Lorraine had been a boy, that might have been it with the
DeMarcos, but Dominic wanted a son fiercely, a son to take
his part in the household of women, a son who would play

football the way Dominic had always wanted to, a son with flash and pizzazz with girls: his son. And in 1954 Josie gave birth to Dominic, Jr., and they called him Sonny.

He was not the son Dominic anticipated, nor the one he wanted. Unable to see Sonny for what he was, Dominic tried relentlessly over the years to change Sonny into a copy of himself. It was not that Dominic didn't love his son. He was simply unable to understand that what he passed on to each of his children was a passion for living life that matched his own, but in a different way in each of them. In short, he wanted himself all over again, particularly in Sonny, a common enough desire in a father, but it became distorted in Dominic. He never let them grow into themselves. He never stopped resenting each of them just a little because they wouldn't live their lives the way *he* thought they should. Anything they did that he opposed he took as a sign of their lack of love and respect. And Sonny's illnesses all through his life, his self-consciousness instead of cockiness, made Dominic nervous. It was unfamiliar to him, and he didn't understand.

When both of the girls left home, Dominic felt the bitterness in him sharpen. Sonny stayed longer than his sisters, but after Josie died, Dominic's need for his son was profound. Unable to express this need, this love (as he had always been unable to express the tenderness in him with anyone except Josie), he turned to riding Sonny's ass about a dozen little things, the way he'd always done. Without Josie to tone Dominic down and stand up for Sonny, Sonny could take no more. He finally lost his temper, a temper he had chewed and swallowed and taken to bed with him for more nights than should have been possible. They had fought plenty before, but in the fight that made Sonny leave home last April, Dominic had raised his hand to strike Sonny, and Sonny, at twenty-six, had at last had enough. He drew back his own fist and punched his father in the mouth, screaming his outrage saved up all these years, screaming in that high-pitched tone his voice took on when he was upset (a detail which infuriated Dominic), screaming and crying and wishing desperately for his mother. His control shot, his head pounding, he had packed a duffle bag of clothes and ran from the house, Dominic screaming all the while: "Get out you miserable son of a bitch. Get out, get out, and don't ever come back." It was the "don't ever come back" that both he and Sonny would remember.

Now it was early November, and Dominic was alone. He woke this morning, a few days before the two-year anniversary of his wife's death, feeling lonely for his Josie and for his kids, pitying himself a bit for how alone he was this day, and thinking hard about his son. For the last couple of weeks he couldn't get the kid off his mind. Sonny had never been away from home before, and Dominic missed him. Lately he had also missed Josie fiercely. He knew that she was angry with him for what had happened between him and Sonny. He rose, thinking, "Okay, Josephine, okay. I'll try to find him. I'll call Rosie. But he can't come home. Unless he says he's sorry. Got no respect."

thirteen

SONNY HAD INSOMNIA. He'd gotten off work at eleven and come straight home. He was quiet, crabby. Moses had been real moody lately, hardly talked to Sonny the last couple of nights. Sonny knew that Moses wasn't feeling well. His skin had taken on a yellowish hue, and he'd been losing weight. This bothered Sonny for a couple of reasons. Over the last eight months, he'd grown attached to Moses, had come to feel that he could talk about things with him that he never mentioned to anyone else, especially about his mother. Sonny knew Moses was getting sick again, or just plain sicker.

It also bothered him in a way he never clearly admitted to himself. His headaches were growing worse, more frequent; the nightmares, too, were increasing. He was almost out of his phenobarbitol and Dilantin. He'd been spacing them out, only taking his medicine twice a day instead of the four times prescribed. It was a prescription refill that meant he had to have a doctor's check-up first. He didn't want to go to Dr. Rizzo and have him ask about his family. Moses' sickness brought up Sonny's problems, and Sonny was trying not to think about them.

Sonny read distractedly for awhile—old *Playboys,* the newspapers—but he was antsy, tense, wide awake. Finally, at

4:00 a.m. he got up, figured he'd go down to the QuikStar and hang out with Moses.

It was a clear night, cold, and Sonny pulled up his collar against the wind. A fire engine was flying down Erie Boulevard and a couple of guys came out of the 7-Eleven to see which way it was headed. Sonny made a small sign of the cross on his forehead, a habit he'd never even attempted to give up. He did the same thing whenever he passed a Catholic church. He went by the phone booth where he called his Momma, already looking forward to the day after tomorrow when he could talk to her again.

The QuikStar was empty, and Moses sat on a red stool with a cup of coffee and a cigarette, looking out the window, thinking. He was glad when he saw Sonny coming in, thought maybe it'd take his mind off things.

"So Mo," Sonny greeted Moses, "what go?" He laughed at himself. The walk over had cheered him up a little. Maybe the cold air cleared his head, or maybe the sight of the phone booth gave him confidence. "Gimme a co-*co*."

Moses groaned and grinned at the same time. Sonny, he thought, where'd he ever come from? "Okay, Sonny boy, coming up. Where you been? Was it good?"

"Better than ever." Sonny said this with an Italian accent. He remembered a great-uncle of his, Tio Gondolfo, who, it seemed to Sonny, only knew three English words. After every meal with Tio someone would say, "So, Tio, was it good?" And he'd say, in very broken English, "Better than ever." Sonny laughed again. "How you doing Moses?"

Moses started to shrug off the question, then stopped himself. "Not good, Sonny. I think it's coming back. My lungs are shot."

"Well," Sonny said, "you don't help it by smoking so much."

"Oh come off it, Sonny, you know it ain't the smoking. I got cancer, man."

Sonny had an impulse to deny this, to say, *Oh c'mon Moses, no you don't.* But he couldn't. "I know. It sucks."

They were both quiet; it didn't seem there was much left to say. The fluorescent light hummed. It was four-thirty in the morning. The light and vacant silence of the hour affected them both. Sonny felt an enormous distance in him open. At just that moment it was as though he and Moses had been abandoned at this counter in the middle of fog, that nothing had ever seemed so desolate, so hopeless, so finished.

The door flew open. It was Ron, his eyes wild, his face and clothes streaked with dirt and soot.

"What the fuck?" Moses was instantly up, on alert. He looked past the door, sure that Ron was being chased for trying to stiff a pimp and they'd all get shot.

Ron stood in the doorway. "Lucinda. I was over to Lucinda's, and the house is on fire."

Sonny had a split second when the entire QuikStar went a violent red. Then he let out a weak groan and fell to the floor in a seizure.

fourteen

HE CAME TO MOANING softly through the spoon Moses was holding in his mouth, holding his tongue forward. He'd only been out a few minutes, enough time to piss his pants and, he was sure, look like an asshole.

"Thatta boy, Sonny, you doin fine. Just rest awhile. It gonna be fine." Moses had slipped a couple of rolled-up aprons under Sonny's head and had taken his glasses off.

Sonny looked up at Moses and let out a short and muffled, but deep sob. Moses leaned over him a little so Ron couldn't see Sonny's face. "You just lay there, Sonny. I'm gonna get you some water."

Sonny turned his head to the side, spotted his glasses, put them on and lay still for a moment. He drank the water Moses offered him, then sat up in the piss-wet pants feeling immensely exhausted. Ron was still standing near the door, looking dumbstruck, and as though he were afraid to move lest he bring on another catastrophe.

Sonny spoke. "Is Lucinda...the baby...are they okay?"

"Lucinda's fine." Ron was out of his daze. "We woke up and the place was filled with smoke, the people next door was screamin, sirens were goin off. She's fine, we got out, but Dawn, she didn't get burned up but this fireman had to give her mouth-to-mouth. They took them to the hospital."

"Who's with Lucinda?" Sonny was agitated. "Who went with her in the ambulance?"

"She went alone, with the baby and some cop."

"You didn't go with her?"

"Sonny, I couldn't go with her with all them cops and everything. They know what she is."

"That be right," Moses spoke softly. "Problem is, Ron, you don't know what *you* is."

"Fuck you two. Shouldnta even come in here. Thought you'd wanna know, Moses. I didn't know you'd be here Sonny, but you oughta wanna know. Dawn's got that stuffed animal you gave her in her crib."

"You're a real asswipe, Ron. Never even made it to the asshole stage. What hospital they go to?"

"Upstate, handsome. But I'd change my pants first if I was you."

Sonny wanted to reply but was growing groggy; he thought dimly that Ron was disgusting, as usual, and then fell into a deep sleep on the QuikStar floor.

fifteen

"ROS-IE, IT'S YOUR FATHER." Dominic, always slightly ill at ease on the telephone with any of his kids (he thought it made him appear needy), affected a kind of teasing whine of a voice. "How the hell've you been?"

"Hi, Pop. Good. How are you? I've been meaning to call you. It's been real busy at work, you know. What have you been doing?" Rose felt a little thrill of tension talking to Dominic. They didn't know each other easily. Every interaction was like with once close friends who meet every year or two: all the habits of familiar intimacy are there, but they have nothing to say beyond those habits.

"I'm good, you know, getting old, that's all. Been hanging around the shop a little. Listen, have you seen your brother?" There, it was out. This, of course, was the reason Dominic had called Rose, but he had to make the right amount of small talk first.

For her part, Rose was glad he brought it up. The second she heard her father's voice she only wanted to ask about Sonny. But she didn't want her father to think she wasn't interested in him, first. "I haven't, Pop. I was going to ask you the same thing. How about Lorraine, do you think she'd know? Do you know how to get a hold of her?"

"Shit." Dominic's voice took on the bitter edge Rose knew well. "Eddie Marino, remember him, the cop used to come over the house with his wife Jeanne, he told me he saw her in one of them malls shopping around Jordan-Elbridge. She told him she was living out there now, in that trailer park, Valley View."

"By herself?" Rose couldn't quite believe that Lorraine would have left the city.

"Ke-rist, Rose, no. Eddie snooped around a little. Found out she's living with Donna and some *melanzana.** I don't know."

"Is she straight now, do you think?"

"Eddie says he thinks so. Said she looked real good, seemed happy enough. He said she asked about me."

"Well, that's good," Rose said. "At least she hasn't forgotten us completely. And the guy's Black? Do you know his name? Did you get her phone number?"

"Yeah. Ya want it? Do me a favor and call her, wouldja? Maybe she's heard from Sonny. I dunno. I doubt it, but let's try."

This phone call was so like Dominic. Rose thought, as she hung up the receiver, that her father had always been that way, had often caused fights and hurt feelings, had said whatever he needed to say, done whatever he'd needed to do, would brood or explode as he needed to; and then, when he began to emerge from his private world or his anger or his bitterness, he would call or appear—warm, caring, ebullient even—and expect everyone to fall back into place. The good place now, not the protected armor that they'd all had to wear during his spells of moodiness. And it was nearly impossible not to respond to this pleasanter Dominic, for his charm was as genuine as his anger could be.

---

*eggplant

But Rose harbored a secret grudge about this, as she suspected her mother must have. Even as she affected a warm voice while talking with him, she was inwardly seething, walking an emotional tightrope: she found it hard to balance the anger he provoked in her with her own need for him in the way he could be, had been just now on the phone. It grated on her, for example, that he hadn't asked one question about herself, her work, not even at the hospital. Yet she offered nothing of her own life to him. She knew that if she did, he'd respond by becoming defensive or rushing off the phone. He was as afraid and resistant of the closeness they might have as she was. Easier, then, to keep the illusion of closeness, to banter, to talk only and most familiarly of family matters. In family matters he'd always turned to Rose, always expecting, and always getting, her complicity.

Here she was again, placed in the position of mediator, of problem solver. Rose the go-between. It seemed to her that it was the one role most often offered her, and it was one that she had taken on and certainly must have encouraged for as long as she could remember. She thought about this now, the years of trying to understand the way everyone else's mind and emotions ran, trying to understand what was required to bring her father around, to bolster Sonny, to talk to Lorraine. It was only with her mother, who demanded little of Rose, that she was most able to be herself — to admit her vulnerability, her fears, her confusions.

With a wry little smile she remembered the one summer she had been allowed to go to Girl Scout day camp. She fell madly in love with the Scout leader. Rose could picture her now. Although she could not remember her name, she could see her red-brown hair, tan poplin skirt, soft beige blouse, and the nylons she wore. She could remember the sound of them as the woman had walked into the campsite, arriving always a quarter hour after the school bus had deposited the campers, about twenty of them — girls from her neighborhood, mostly Italians, a few Germans — and then the leader.

Rose thought now she must have been English, and she, having just read *Little Women* and *Jane Eyre,* she at twelve beginning to float in that wonderful and terrifying haze where everything is riveting in its sensuality, where legs and breasts and pubic hair (peach fuzz, or feathers, her mother called it) seem to shiver or tingle or emphasize the self all out of proportion, she remembered how she ached for the sight of the leader coming down a small grassy hill shaded by oaks and pines just off the parking lot. She could recall with detail the sensation of fire she had, and the burning awareness that the woman knew what Rose was feeling, and that no one else had even a glimmer of knowing.

And then the play, the highlight of the summer, when they dressed in costume and invited their families and friends and could show off to their heart's content. It was a play about the early settlers. She was chosen by the woman who made her heart pound to play John Alden, to carry Miles Standish's declaration of love to the sensitive Priscilla, who says, of course, "Speak for yourself, John."

It seemed to Rose that always, even in play, this had been her job: to speak for others, to carry their messages, to avoid herself. It was a job she finally was wearying of, and she struggled to cast it off. She found this hard to do — even a little alarming to do — for without it, she was a very new and different Rose. In many ways Rose and Sonny shared a similar kind of emotionality, but it was as though Rose had begun to see it, to understand it, to use it now more and more in her photographs, in herself. She had come to a place in her life where she had developed past an unquestioning acceptance of what she knew, had always known about emotion, about people and their ways, and she wanted to keep it now for herself.

Her mother had often said to her when she was growing up: "There's two things, Rosie, ya gotta watch: your tongue is too quick, it's your worst enemy, and you're selfish." Those words had struck home for Rose. She'd resisted them, but recognizing some truth, she strove to be more silent, to not giggle in church, to not always have a better story than the others. She gave things away, thinking this would make her mother see she was generous. But Josephine's meaning of selfish, Rose was beginning to understand had nothing to do with the material world. Josephine had watched Rosie refuse Lorraine her hand when Lorraine was afraid to cross the street, or tell her sister stories that terrified her until she cried; and Rose could taunt "Ba-by, Ba-by" until Josephine had to slap her good. It was a side of herself Rose hated, was ashamed of, but one she recognized. Perhaps it was her way, first as a kid and even as a woman, to preserve some part of her, to assert that yes, she would try to make peace, make nice, but she wasn't without her own need for attention, for being seen for herself, flawed if also giving.

One of the recent flaws had been avoiding looking for Sonny, something she'd known she should have done since that day in July when she'd gone to the cemetery. She could no longer blame it on the relationship with Deborah, for in the last couple of months they had finally reached some degree of calm. They saw each other several times a week, and Rose had let go of the compelling need she'd had to possess Deborah. For her part, Deborah had stopped drinking, had been sober for a full two months, enough past the danger point she'd always had of two good weeks before showing up one night drunk and mean, or drunk and self-pitying. In fact, Deborah had been pushing on Rose to try and locate Sonny.

She had developed a little bit of a soft spot for him, having recognized in the couple of dinners the three of them had had together something of his deep sense of futility.

Rose would almost always bristle when Deborah brought it up. "I *will*," she'd say. "I told you I will. You just don't understand." When Deborah would ask what was it she didn't understand, Rose would be deliberately evasive. "The whole thing, the whole situation, you just don't understand." But Rose understood. She knew she couldn't face it, couldn't face the possibility that Sonny might need help. Rose knew her avoidance was an example of just the kind of selfishness her mother warned her against. And couldn't—didn't want to—change it. She could feel the fragile wings of her just recently attained self-harmony begin to tremble and shake and threaten to fly off, leaving her once again bereft of the only thing she was learning to count on: her own passion.

She sat at her kitchen counter after she'd hung up the phone, looking at herself in the mirror over the sink, noticing again the gray that was thickening in her dark brown, almost black hair. She looked at the widow's peak on her forehead, the cleft in her chin, seeing herself and her father's face at once in those things. And her eyes—large and round, almost pupil-less in their darkness—so like her mother's. The same eyes that both Lorraine and Sonny looked out from. She thought of her family and the ties she felt to each of them despite their long distances from one another. She sat staring at the phone number in her hand, thinking how long it had been since she'd seen Lorraine, remembering the last time—at her mother's funeral and Lorraine very pregnant. She knew she had a niece or a nephew she'd never laid eyes on and that, if her father's information from Eddie Marino was right, the baby was half-Black. She remembered that Lorraine had looked okay at the funeral, not that haggard, yellowish tint to her skin like in the old days; that Lorraine had tried to talk to

Rose, and Rose had brushed her off. And thinking about that, about her only sister and her own refusal to come close to her, Rose felt a familiar sensation begin in her gut—a warmth unpleasant, like shame or guilt. She hesitated only another minute, lighting a cigarette, ignoring the need in herself to cry, before she picked up the phone and dialed Lorraine's number.

sixteen

JUNIOR WRAPPED HIMSELF around Rose's legs as she sat at the small table in Lorraine and Curtis's trailer, drinking coffee and taking in the fact that her sister had been off drugs for almost four years. This was much longer than Rose had allowed as a possibility, a fact that threatened to bring up that scalding guilt again. But she fought it down. It was out of place here — here, today, with Lorraine looking more relaxed than Rose could ever remember seeing her. The trailer sat on a site toward the rear of the park, and while most of the trailer park had been stripped of foliage, through the kitchen window she and Lorraine looked out on trees and the birds that flocked to the several feeders Lorraine had out. The kitchen was tiny, wood-paneled, decorated in orange and browns, and had the kind of disarray that told of a family living in a small space. They drank from orange mugs with brown kittens on them; over the table hung three small paintings of cats, all gifts from Sonny over the years.

Donna was at school, Curtis at work. She and Lorraine were quiet at first, a little shy, and Junior, warming immediately as he did to Rose, gave them a safe topic of conversation. He was a wiry little guy, brown skinned, his long-lashed eyes gleaming. Rose took him in, lifting him up onto her lap, and said to Lorraine, "How old is he now?"

Lorraine grinned, fished a cigarette from her shirt pocket. "He'll be two on the twenty-ninth of this month. He was born right after Momma's funeral. I was going to call you Rosie, but I figured you'd be too busy. You didn't seem interested in anything much then."

"I don't know Lorraine. I guess I was blown away about Momma. Sometimes I still can't believe it." She paused. "And I know I just assumed you were still on drugs."

For just a second, Lorraine's dark eyes blazed darker. "Why didn't you ask, Rosie, instead of just assuming? I know that's what you thought. That's the real reason I didn't call. You all held me to that place, and I guess it just sorta pissed me off."

Rose played with Junior's hair; he leaned against her, dozing. "Well," she said, "I guess we all just avoid each other when there's something that really needs to get talked about. But...Lorraine...." She hesitated, a little embarrassed as she always was when she had to admit she was wrong, or when she was trying to make things feel right again. She looked up at her sister, wanting Lorraine to make it easier for her. And, like the easygoing creature Lorraine had always been, she did.

"Ah, forget it, Rosie. You called, you're here now. Junior likes you, and he's not that friendly with most people. Will you stay for dinner? Curtis'll be home in about an hour. We're having meat loaf."

Rose hesitated, more out of habit than desire. She felt an old pull tug at her. She could see Deborah tonight since they both had the weekend off, or she could stay here knowing that staying was probably going to make her feel the same way she had felt all her adult life when she was around Lorraine or Sonny: that she was the one who had really split from her family, that everything about her was different from them. She tortured herself with this knowledge. And then she felt at once snobbish and so happy to be home — to *be* — to not have to worry about the world she was now a part of. Even as she thought this her eyes were scanning the bookcase-divider separating the kitchen and living room, seeing Lorraine's books. There were so many familiar titles among them. Then her eyes moved back to the kitchen table where *The Color Purple* rested atop the toaster oven, a book Rose had just started herself. Rose remembered that she and Lorraine had read the same books, had shared a politics and an awareness of inequalities in the world that was part of their growing up Italian. Rose had always made something of these tastes, giving them a special significance, forgetting that Lorraine just lived them in her own private and honest way. Again, that warm unpleasantness; again, she willed it away.

"I'd love to stay. Thanks, Lorraine." And she meant it, as thanks not just for the dinner invitation, but for the graceful way which Lorraine let Rose back in, straight from her heart; for the way Lorraine knew instinctively to let go of the past because this moment right here felt good. "Do you think Curtis will like me?"

He did, but he also took more in than he offered. He knew the hurt Lorraine had felt because of Rose's coolness to her; he knew also that it was important for Lorraine to get back in touch with her family. His own family had helped them out, and they saw them often. Once they got past an initial disappointment that Curtis was with a white girl, they took to Lorraine and she to them. They had lent Curtis and Lorraine the down payment for the trailer, and Mildred Fuller watched Junior and Donna for them sometimes for the weekend so that "the kids" could go fishing up to the north country every once in awhile. Curtis was a tall man, slender and quiet. He'd worked at Crucible Steel since he graduated from high school. He clearly was Junior's idol, and even Donna seemed to have warmed to Curtis, certainly more than she did to Rose at this little reunion.

When Donna came in from school, Rose had seen the look — first of surprise, then wariness — that crossed her face. Rose wondered how Lorraine had explained her family's absence, even on holidays, to Donna. Whatever the explanation had been, it was clear that Donna, at seventeen, was going to make up her own mind. She came in carrying an armful of schoolbooks, wearing Calvin Klein jeans and a pink LaCoste sweater, tossing her long blonde hair back slightly, caressing the curling iron waves, taking in all of Rose in one long, intense look. After she said hello, she wanted to know just one thing: "Have you seen Uncle Sonny?" Donna loved Sonny. Though she hadn't seen him often, there was something particularly sweet in her memory of him; perhaps it was his gentleness with her, or the way he had always talked with her, naturally.

When Rose told Lorraine on the phone that Sonny had been away from home, that neither she nor their father had heard from him since April, Lorraine had not seemed too worried. Lorraine always had thought that Sonny was watched too closely, that he hadn't been permitted to express much of what he was within the family.

"You know Sonny, Rosie," she said now, "he was always real private about himself, and God knows it was hard enough to get any privacy at home. Phones always ringing, people in and out. And there's Sonny hiding out in his room when Poppa didn't make him go down to the shop." She stopped, rolled up her eyes. "If that wasn't the craziest idea Poppa ever had, trying to turn Sonny into a truck driver."

Rose grinned. "Yeah, well at least he also came up with the idea to let Sonny dispatch. He had to do something, Lorraine."

"I guess. What could he be doing now, how do you think he's making a living? And those seizures. Jesus, Rosie, when I think about that, ya know, I just wonder if he's driving, or what. Where could he live? I don't think he even has any friends he could be staying with."

"I don't know. He's pretty good about taking his pills. All I really know is that he and Poppa had a fight in April, something about Poppa getting on Sonny about little stuff. You know, the laundry, that he should put in more hours at ADS. Pop said Sonny lost his temper and hit him, so he threw him out. Of course when Pop told me, he made it sound like Sonny was just crazy mad, as though he hadn't done anything to warrant Sonny's outburst. But," she shrugged, "you know Poppa and *his* temper. I had talked to Sonny a couple of weeks before, and he sounded okay. When Poppa told me about the fight, I just figured same as you—maybe he has to be alone for awhile. Then the violet was at Momma's grave. I keep thinking maybe he'll call, or even show up on the twenty-first."

"Yeah, but Rosie, remember how Sonny was when Momma died? I don't know that we should hope for him showing up at the anniversary mass or anything like that. I don't think Sonny ever got used to Momma's dying. He was a mess at the funeral, like he was in a fog, stumbling around. I thought he was drunk or stoned or something."

Rose ran a hand through her hair, thinking. Lorraine was right. Sonny had gone into a real tailspin after Momma died. It was so fast, Rose thought, nobody had time to get ready. But Sonny had an intense reaction. He'd been sick to his stomach and had one of the worst headaches Rose could remember him having, and he slept whole days. A couple of times he'd seemed out of it to Rose; he didn't seem to remember that Momma was dead when he woke up. Rose figured he was truly in shock. She knew how hard it was for Sonny to be

without Momma. It was hard for her too, for all of them, but
Sonny was the hardest hit. It probably was a mistake to think
of him showing up on the twenty-first, but at least it gave
Rose something to hope for. She said, "You're probably right
Lorraine. Unless he's better about it by now. Anyway the anniversary mass is a week from tomorrow. Let's just hope he's
there."

"What if he isn't? What do you think we should do?"

"I don't know. Same as we're doing now, I guess. Keep
hoping he'll call. I don't even know where to begin looking.
Any ideas?"

Lorraine thought for a minute, and then she grinned at
Rose. "Well," she said, "Poppa could talk to his pals on the
police force. Eddie Marino found out a whole lot about me
real fast. All I told him was I lived out here so you and Poppa
would at least know that—I guess I was hoping you'd call,
Rosie—but, Jesus, I should think Poppa could try to get
some of those guys to keep an eye out."

"I don't think so, Lorraine. Poppa doesn't want anybody
to know. He had to tell Uncle Tony and Uncle Sal, of course,
but he doesn't want anybody out of the family to know that
Dominic DeMarco can't find his only son. If anybody asks,
he probably says he moved out, is on his own now. Besides,
I'd hate to have people snooping on Sonny. It'd drive him
nuts, don't you think?"

They had dinner, and the talk shifted to lighter topics.
Over coffee Lorraine pulled out photo albums filled with pictures of her family. Before she left, Rose took her own
photographs of Lorraine, Curtis, Donna, and Junior. Seeing
them through the lens of her camera, she felt a tug in her
chest, trying to capture on film a closeness she ached for.

seventeen

OH YES, AND THE FUMBLING *at her blouse that last night. Unsure of himself as always, the fine lines across his forehead
going deeper in the moment he knew he wanted to touch her
and that she was going to let him, his heart throbbing with the
sense of it; his longing like a sad thing, dense and thick and
certain of not failure or rejection but that old rumbling sense
of inadequacy. And as he fumbled, opened her blouse and let
his hand roam across her breast, the gesture not giving him
away just yet. At the touch of her skin his hand moved almost
as a thing apart from himself; for it moved with certainty. All
the time the motion of his mind traveling far from his body,
and his body responding to suspense and the softest skin he
thought he had ever known and her nipple now firm under
his finger and he leaned to kiss her and did kiss her. It was as
though it was someone else there with Linda till he rocked
himself shut in his head, moved till that pounding came in his
chest, and he knew too fast who he was. Suddenly he saw his
own face collapsing in the need for this touching, his eyes flat
in an instant, and he pulled away from her, withdrew his
hand, grew silent, immutable. Linda, perplexed again by his
withdrawal, curled into herself on the couch in her apartment
and didn't try this time to probe him. She just left him sitting
in his familiar silence grim-faced, while inside of himself Sonny recognized only the despair. He would not say failure*

because this had always been his successful finish. Always this return only to himself. The old distance he had learned to create for himself around all those he loved except Momma, who had never endangered him but understood— the quiet, the need to retreat in herself, also. Great waves of this distance engulfed him now as he sat on the same couch as Linda, despising himself a little, for he wanted her even now. Still aroused and wanting her in his body which seemed to him too far away from what his insides were saying to ever hear that other language in a way that would make translation.

Something brought this memory back to Sonny in his post-seizure sleep, the way he'd been thinking about Lucinda—or something in the way he felt thinking about Lucinda—when for an instant opened to his own need, his desire. Without ever saying the words, Sonny knew that he wanted, and it had been a very long time since he had felt that. It created in him a sense of danger, rubbing as it did against his resignation to isolation. Sonny had never sought the aloneness he lived with. The recognition he had of being alone had, in its own way, created him. It had shaped his habits, all carefully geared to keeping him away from his need, away from emotion and its potential for havoc.

Sonny knew the great space of his loneliness, felt it wider than Lake Ontario, stretching in places beyond his vision. He knew its motion like that of the big lake and tried to rock himself in it night after night, with his headaches or his sadness, alive to his need only in privacy when something small would catch it off guard: a strain of music from a neighbor's radio, or the gray light filtering into his room mid-winter, midday, or the smell of cedar that sometimes rose off telephone poles on rainy days when he'd remember something he had no words for.

And it didn't matter, it didn't matter. Sonny felt in himself an old ache rise, familiar as breath, and it was a breath he had grown to hate in himself. Yet he needed it. It was the only thing that made any sense to him.

He lay there, he got up, he smelled himself on his pants, he thought of what he could do. He could go to the hospital, catch up with Lucinda, convince her to stay at his place; or he could go home as usual and flop into bed, exhausted. Even now his head was beginning to pound again, reminding him of how seldom he had been seen for himself, and he wanted to cry. Over near the counter Moses stood nursing still another cup of coffee, watching Sonny or drifting in his own world out the window. Sonny looked at Moses and knew that even *he* was in himself, and it seemed to Sonny that he was the only one who understood something no one else came close to. His heart beat furiously. His head ached and ached, and in him was the deepest sadness. It had been there all along, but it was new, too, and it was so large, so sad to him in that moment that he was alone.

Sonny was alone in his piss-stained pants, his belly hanging over the edge of them. He saw himself as Moses must have seen him, and every sadness he'd ever known came to him as he lay there. He tried to control himself, for there were people around. He wasn't at home and had nothing to fall back on here. Still, Sonny couldn't keep himself from crying. The tears, large and uncontained, splashed on his face. He rubbed them away, feeling his own whiskers harsh against his fingers when he longed for something soft, something to take a little of what he was feeling away, to smooth out for him the sharp edges of himself so he could be the way he was when he first came into the QuikStar — happy, making jokes.

But Sonny felt only loneliness as he lay there. He was flooded with the memories of every mistake he'd ever made; each time he'd been the fool; each time his face had been there — naked, exposed, vulnerable — and he wanted to die then, just die on the floor of the QuikStar. There was nothing to save of himself except the spirit that lived in him that even now tormented him with what it knew, with what he, Sonny, knew, and he couldn't die just yet. He couldn't.

He thought of his Momma and how she would feel knowing Sonny was ready to give up, lying there like a beached whale, and the thought of her — her face, her eyes, dreamy and hopeful at once — came up to him, rose up off the floor and entered him, and he knew that the day after tomorrow he could call her. He knew that she wanted him, she above all, that no one else had ever seen into him, and he saw her face urging him gently up, past this small moment in time as he knew it. He saw it and was calmed temporarily, as though the feeling in his chest that had been beating like a bird with its wings crazed had relaxed, and his heart slowed. It was only the pounding in his head that wouldn't stop, but his chest stopped its fluttering. He fell back against the aprons, accepting himself as he knew his Momma would have, fell back, slept, waited in his dreaming for this moment, too, to pass.

◆

Moses woke him at 6:00 a.m. He took a cab home, pulling his coat tight around himself. He had to go home, be by himself. He couldn't risk what little spirit was left in him. His head throbbed; his eyes were distant and dreamy, the pupils enormous. Sonny was so far inside a single sensation that it was as though it was the only one he'd ever known, the only one he would ever know. It was a kind of riveting sadness that pulsated with its own force of energy, beating most profoundly in his head. The veins in his temples jumped with it, and yet he felt himself distant from it, removed from any physical sensation of pain. This was Sonny's shield, his safety, his never-failing method of protecting himself. But it was only the outside that he was protected from. At times like these Sonny would have been better off to push himself through the moments of utter despair, for no one else would ever be as hard on Sonny as he was on himself.

He paid the cabby, stumbled up the stairs to his apartment, opened the door, and entered the room. He smelled the slightly musty odor of his rooms, craved the darkened living room, the feel of the naugahyde couch, anything that was now only his. He would cry, but first he had to feel himself home, feel himself out of danger, and the fluttering of danger still hovered in the air around him. It urged him further inside himself until the cold took hold in his belly and moved on up through his body. Slowly, the fluttering stopped. He reached up and brushed the hair away from his forehead, and it was that—the feel of his own hand on his face, his own fingers tender on his head and the memory of touching, of another hand touching—that did it. Sonny let himself go, felt raw need in him explode in a burst of sorrow. He sat there alone on the red couch sobbing for something unnameable and so simple in its agony that it alarmed him, added another edge to his sadness that he didn't understand but only felt with his whole body aching.

He slept and dreamt, dim dreams of his Momma calling to him, vague colors moving him in and out of sleep. Yet when he awoke he remembered nothing. Sonny still had a headache, though the pounding was not as constant. It was Saturday, and it was already one-thirty in the afternoon. He hadn't gotten home from the QuikStar till close to 7:00 a.m. He awoke ravenously hungry and feeling curiously bruised, tender, as though he had the flu, but he didn't feel sick in that way. He stood in the shower for a long time, running the hot water over him, trying to shake the fogginess from his mind, trying to think what he should do. He wasn't going to work; Moses told him he'd take his shift. He could eat, dress, and race over to the hospital to see Lucinda and Dawn. He figured he was more likely to catch up with them there. He doubted Lucinda would be at home — if she could even stay at her own house — unless something had happened to the baby, or unless the baby was fine. And it was Saturday. Rose hardly ever worked weekends.

When he came out of the shower, he reached, as he always did, for his pills. It was then the memory of the seizure came back full force. He had pushed it off to the back of his mind, hadn't wanted to think about it. But he thought of it now, swallowing his pills with a gulp of lukewarm coffee. Sonny didn't want to call Dr. Rizzo, but he wanted to have another seizure even less: they terrified him. He had a deep fear that he wouldn't wake up from one of them, and he hated not knowing what he looked like when he was out cold. He had enough pills for only another few days. Sonny stood there with a towel wrapped around himself, his glasses sliding slowly down his wet nose, trying to figure out what to do. He fixed pepperoni and eggs, had another cup of coffee, and got dressed.

Once outside in the cold gray afternoon air, he stopped at his phone booth and called Dr. Rizzo. He scheduled an appointment for Monday morning. That put it off for awhile and took care of it at the same time. Now he could head for Upstate.

eighteen

ALL THE WHILE Sonny had been going through first his insomnia and then his reaction to the fire, Lucinda Potts had been sweating it out in the Emergency Room of Upstate. Someone had run for her mother, God knows why, and Charlotte Potts rolled into Emergency a couple of hours after Lucinda and Dawn had. She was a skinny, nervous looking woman, still dressed in her nightgown with a tan raincoat over it, eyes darting all around, constantly sniffing, and she was carrying a large bag. Lucinda heard her mother before she saw her.

"Now look here," Charlotte was saying, "my daughter and my grandchild are here someplace. Where they be? You tell me now."

Lucinda came out of the waiting room and headed for the desk. She knew what had happened. Probably the night clerk thought Charlotte looked more like a patient than a visitor and wasn't going to release any information till Charlotte produced her Medicaid card. No doubt Charlotte hadn't even told them who her daughter and her grandchild were. That was Charlotte: swift as a knife on the street, but totally unable to survive in any part of the regulated system. She just didn't understand the rules, and even if she did, she sure as shit wouldn't trust them—she knew they weren't made for her. Lucinda knew this because she had that in her, too. Difference was, even though she played about as far outside the rules anybody could play, she had taken the time to get the regular rules to work, if not *for* her, then at least she tried to avoid them going against her. She'd had to learn that in her business, and it served her well; she'd never yet been picked up for hooking.

"Here I am, Ma. How did you find out about the fire?" Lucinda looked beat. She'd come to the hospital in the robe and slippers she'd thrown on when they smelled the smoke. Her eyes were red and swollen, some from the smoke she took in, some from the crying and worrying about Dawn she'd done since she'd been here.

"Adora Delight came for me. Said you might need some clothes. Look like you do. Where the baby at?"

"She's in x-ray. She was hardly breathing when we got here, but they brought her back. They had to use this little bag to help her breathe, Ma, she turned so dark. But they say she's gonna be okay now. They wanna keep her for twenty-four hours, make sure she don't get pneumonia or something. What else did Adora say?"

Adora lived in the apartment next to Lucinda. They weren't great friends — Adora's style was flashier than Lucinda's — but they helped each other in and out of jams.

"Nothin. Cept that you was with some white boy who disappeared faster than a shadow in shade when the fire broke out. I tol ya, Lucinda, stay with your own."

"Sure, Ma." Lucinda was in no mood for this old argument. Anyways, she couldn't see where her mother was any better off just dealing with their kind. She wondered what some of her mother's customers would do if they were making a buy at Charlotte's when a fire broke out. Wasn't no use arguing about it now. She was okay. Dawn was going to be okay, far as they knew. "Thanks for bringing the clothes. I'm gonna go in the bathroom and put em on. You gonna stay?"

"Well, I'll stay till I see the baby. But it's eight-thirty, and I gotta meet somebody back home in about an hour."

"Okay, c'mon, I'll show you where to wait." She got her mother settled in the waiting room, brought her a cup of coffee from a machine, and went off to change her clothes. Lucinda came back wearing a pair of bluejeans that were a little too big—Adora outweighed her by at least fifteen pounds—an orange Syracuse University sweatshirt, and white sneakers. Adora had also put a ten dollar bill in the bag. When she got to the waiting room, Charlotte was gone. Lucinda shrugged her shoulders, shook her head, and sat down to wait for Dawn to get back from x-ray.

◆

They didn't get Dawn properly admitted to the pediatric ward until close to noon. After the x-rays, they did some more blood tests, then took another x-ray, and finally made the arrangements to move her up the children's unit. Dawn was beginning to look like herself again. Her own color had returned, and though she slept, she looked more likely to wake up than she had when they first arrived. Her breathing sounded nice and easy, not the awful rasping she was doing at first.

A nurse came up and told Lucinda to follow her. She brought Dawn to a room with four cribs in it. None of the others were filled. The nurse got Dawn all settled. She changed her diapers and covered her with a little white blanket. Then she said to Lucinda, "You must be exhausted. Why don't you go home for a couple of hours? She's going to be fine now." She smiled. The nurse seemed nice enough; at least she talked to Lucinda like she was real. She put out her hand. "I'm Marie Rogers. I'll be watching Dawn until three, when the shift changes. If you have any questions, ask me, okay? And really, if you want to leave for a little while, or just go get something to eat, I think it's safe now. Just tell me where you are, so if we need you for anything we can find you."

Lucinda shook Marie Rogers' hand. "I'm Lucinda Potts. Dawn's my only baby. I got no reason to leave, but I am hungry. Maybe I'll go get a sandwich and bring it back here."

"Sure," Marie said. "The snack bar's on the first floor. Just take the elevator to one. You can't miss it. And I'll get you if anything comes up. You can relax a little."

"Yeah, maybe I will. You the head nurse here Miss Rogers?"

"You can call me Marie, Lucinda. No, Rose DeMarco is the head nurse. She's off today, so I'm in charge."

"Rose DeMarco? She got a brother named Sonny?"

"Yes. Why, do you know him?"

Something in Marie Rogers' manner made Lucinda immediately sorry she asked. Marie's eyebrows had drawn together just a bit, and as she asked Lucinda why she leaned forward a little. "No," Lucinda lied. "A friend of mine used to work with somebody named Sonny DeMarco. But that was a long time ago. The name just stuck, I guess." She paused, then got up, looked at Dawn sleeping in the crib, touched her face, and said, "I *am* gonna go get some lunch, Marie. Thank you."

Walking toward the elevator Lucinda wondered what had made the change in Marie Rogers when she asked about Sonny. Lucinda wasn't even sure what made her ask. Sonny never did say much about himself or his family. She shrugged to herself, thinking oh well, no harm done, and reminding herself to tell Sonny about it next time she saw him.

She didn't have long to wait. She ate a tuna fish sandwich, had a cup of coffee and a cigarette in the snack bar. She took a little time now knowing that Dawn was okay, and that the nurse seemed nice enough. She savored the last few puffs on her cigarette, trying to figure out what she would do when she left the hospital. She couldn't stay with her mother, and Adora Delight's place was probably burned out too. Maybe she'd just have to move into a new place. The thought of that made her groan. She'd only lived on West Colvin six months. She stubbed out her cigarette and left the snack bar, walking slowly toward the elevator.

There stood Sonny, leaning against the wall across from the elevator, waiting. Lucinda felt a little warmth move in her chest for a second: Sonny, she thought, of course.

Lucinda was not a believer in myth or romance, but she understood need, and something of friendship. She'd been disappointed when her mother disappeared from the waiting room. She felt as though the events of the past day had worked on her till she was stripped of almost all her strength. Both Ron and Charlotte had taken from her, and left her—especially Ron. That she could stand. She expected little more from each of them, although she still had wanted something more from her mother.

And Dawn. For a split second earlier she had thought for sure that Dawn was going to be taken from her, too; that she would also leave her. In that moment she had experienced a sense of distance—enormous and vacant—and she thought: this is the view of my life. In the middle of the night, in November, an icy rainy snow beginning to fall as the ambulance careened toward the Emergency Room. Dawn going gray and gasping for breath in that awful way. Lucinda alone, half-naked in an ambulance, the attendants taking good enough care of Dawn but giving each other looks, their pale eyes swooping over Lucinda like skittish birds, their faces pasty in the eerie light of the ambulance at night. And she, thinking, what is it? Why is this happening? Not in a way that questioned why it was happening to *her,* or to Dawn. It was a bigger why. A why for which she knew there was no answer except for randomness, the way things just happen to people.

Look at Moses, she thought, just going about living his life and getting sick like that out of the blue. Or like that guy, a cop, the one she read about during the summer, who walked into J.C. Penney's where his wife worked, and in the middle of the afternoon in the furniture section in a big mall pulled out his gun and shot himself and his wife dead, and nobody'll ever know why. Or like Dawn being the one to almost die. Lucinda knew it wasn't some punishment for how she lived her life; it was just that Dawn was the sickest from it. That was just the way it was. Even Sonny. She knew that Sonny walked around with some sort of sorrow in him; she didn't need any details to understand that. Sonny was too tuned in to the hurts of the few people around him to not carry his own, as Lucinda guessed most everybody did — but hardly anybody copped to it.

Sonny was off somewhere else in his head as he stood leaning against the wall of the hospital gift shop, hands jammed into his pockets, his eyes downcast, waiting for the elevator. He had a slight headache. The back of his neck felt tense, tingly, and his eyes hurt if he raised them. A lab technician walked by, swinging a basket over the side of her arm. The smell of alcohol drifted up as she moved by. Sonny smelled it and a sensation, like a memory that hurt, seeped into his chest. He drew up his right hand under his coat to his solar plexus and stood there trying to touch it away.

Her hand felt papery, too thin. He could see tiny blue veins on her hands as he took them in his own. A lab technician, a little blood. His Momma saying, Oh Sonny, her eyes dark, intense and burning, her face looking dry and white, her breathing sorry and mournful as a small breeze just before dawn. What is it, he said, what is it, Momma? Don't forget, Sonny, don't forget. Forget what? he said. Don't forget to feed the birds, Sonny, and she had reached up and touched his face, her hand fluttery and dry. And then her hand had drifted to his chest, her hand pulling at his shirt till she touched his skin. Here she said, here Sonny. Then she was sleeping again, her breath easier.

"Sonny?" Lucinda reached up and touched Sonny's shoulder gently. She knew he hadn't seen her yet; she knew he was here to see her and Dawn.

He jumped, tried to recover. "Whataya trying to scare me to death? You okay? Dawn?" His voice sounded rough, and he cleared his throat. His eyes were cloudy. He shook his head a little.

"Fine. We're both fine now. Dawn had a bad time at first, but she's okay now. She's up on pediatrics. How are you? Who told you?"

"Ron." Sonny said no more, but his face tensed as he said the name. His eyes darkened. "I'm fine. Moses is covering for me at the Star. Can I come with you to see Dawn?"

"Sure, Sonny." Then Lucinda remembered Marie Rogers. "But Sonny, do you know some nurse up there named Marie Rogers? I asked who was head nurse. She, this Marie, said Rose DeMarco was, and I don't know why, but I asked if she was any kin to you. This Marie said yes, and I don't know, Sonny, she seemed a little nosy about you to me. So anyway, she's up there." Lucinda wasn't sure why she sensed that something about Rose DeMarco and this Marie Rogers meant some kind of trouble for Sonny. She didn't even really want to think about it, but something about Sonny made her want to let him know, wanted to try to help him out, if help was what was needed.

"I met her once." Sonny remembered a party Rose had given at the house a few years ago, a Christmas party for the staff of pediatrics, Marie Rogers among them. "It's okay. Just don't mention anything about the QuikStar or anything else, all right? I'll tell you about it sometime. Let's go see Dawn."

"Okay, Sonny." She paused, looked at him and said, "Thanks for coming."

nineteen

ROSE HAD CALLED Deborah from Lorraine's and asked her to meet her back at her place. They were enjoying a rare Saturday together, free from work, both relaxed and happier than they'd been in awhile. Rose was feeling expansive; the night with Lorraine and Curtis and the kids gave her the sense that things could be okay between them all again.

Early afternoon sunlight broke through the gray skies of the morning and filtered into Rose's room. The two of them lay in bed, propped up on orange pillows, under a brown down quilt, listening to a Pat Metheny tape, pleasantly stoned. Rose was admiring Deborah's dark brown hair, streaked with gray now, a fact which delighted Rose. She ran her fingers through it. "You know, Deb," she paused, turned Deborah's face toward her so she was looking directly at her, "I love your hair." She bent her head to kiss it.

"And," Deborah smiled, "I love you when you're like this. You should see Lorraine more often."

"Yeah, how about it? I think it's going to be okay now. Just wish we could find Sonny by the twenty-first."

"Well, if you try to find him you will. I mean, he must be in Syracuse." Deborah lit a cigarette, took a sip of coke and passed it to Rose. "Don't you think? Where else could he be? And it's not *that* big a town. Did Lorraine have any ideas?"

"Not really." Rose took a drag from Deborah's cigarette. "She thought that maybe as a last resort we could ask Eddie Marino to check around. I don't know. I don't think my father would go for that too big. But if we don't hear from Sonny soon, I guess that's the only thing to do. What do you think?"

The tape ended. Deborah stretched her lean arms up over her head and sighed contentedly. "I think you'll find him or hear from him soon. You've started the ball in motion. I think I'm going to turn the tape over. You roll another joint."

She got up, and Rose watched her walk across the room, the light touching her body, its firm and delicate contours — the slight round to her belly, her back slender, broadening just slightly at her shoulders. Rose loved the arc of those shoulders, the line of her neck, the way the sunlight played on the tiny golden hairs, making Deborah's skin shimmer. She turned over the tape and walked back to the bed. Rose thought she could watch Deborah move forever and never get tired of it. Her breasts small, full, the nipples hard in the coolness of the room, the very light pinkness of them. And Deborah, knowing how Rose watched her, moved slowly across the room.

She got back into bed. They smoked the joint, listening to the music, quiet, next to one another, thighs touching. Deborah reached up and put her arm around Rose. "This is nice," she said grinning. "I love you a lot today, Rosie."

Rose grinned back. "You do, huh?"

They turned on their sides and lay facing each other. Rose kissed Deborah. "I love you too," she said, running her hand along Deborah's side, touching her lightly at first. She took her breast in her hand, feeling the soft and tender skin like something of her own body, and Deborah's hands on her back, on her thighs, on her breasts. Rose moved slowly for the pleasure of this touching. She brought her mouth down to

Deborah's breast and took it in her mouth, her tongue moving around her nipple, her hand stroking her belly, feeling the soft and springy pubic hair, and through it, to the center, to the very center of her. Rose's hand moved slowly, felt Deborah grow wet, opening to her. Now she was inside her and could feel the soft and wonderful dampness of the woman she loved on her fingers. Rose touched her, kissed her mouth again, still inside her, and Deborah looked up at her. Their eyes linked, and she moved against Rose's fingers. Rose raised herself up on an elbow for a second to look at Deborah, the fullness of her, at the light on her body, and then brought her mouth down to Deborah, her wetness on her face like a dream, like a wonderful dream of pleasure. Kissing her belly, her hands on her breasts, her face, her tongue on the wetness that was Deborah, her tongue inside her, feeling her tongue on the inside of her. Then up, stroking her with her tongue, her fingers inside her, feeling her hard under her tongue and so pliant on her fingers. Her other hand on her breast, now on her face, and Deborah moving with her, first slowly, then faster. Rose lifted her eyes up to see her face in the sunlight, and Deb came full against her mouth, her tongue, her fingers. Rose stayed there another moment, inside of her, feeling Deborah's heartbeat on her mouth, feeling her open and close, open and close, loving her more than she'd ever loved in her lifetime, and then bringing her face up, wet with Deborah, to kiss her full on the mouth. Deborah pulled Rose's head closer to her own, returning that kiss, resting a moment before she moved her own hand down the length of Rose's body till she was home, and they moved again, making love again, slowly, as the light began its shifting.

When the phone rang at four o'clock they were both dozing, curved into each other, Deborah facing Rose's back with her arms around her, holding her breasts.

"Oh shit," Rose groaned.

"Don't answer it, Rosie." Deborah pulled Rose closer.

"I have to. Just in case it's Sonny or something about Sonny."

"Mmmm," was all she heard back from Deborah.

Rose reached for the phone. "Hello," she said, trying not to sound groggy. She lit a cigarette.

"Rose. Hi, it's Marie."

"Oh, hi Marie, what's up? Got a problem on the floor?"

"No, no problems there. But listen, I don't know if this means anything, but I know you said you hadn't heard from Sonny in awhile, and we had this admission today, a baby with smoke inhalation, and her mother — her name is Lucinda Potts — asked who the head nurse was. When I said your name, she wanted to know if you had a brother named Sonny. I said yes. Then she sort of backed off, said she just knew *of* him. And then, about an hour later, she showed up on the floor with him. I was going to call you, but we got a couple of admissions in a row, and Fran Coley called in sick today. He only stayed about twenty minutes."

"You saw Sonny?" Rose was wide awake, puffing away on her cigarette. She nudged Deborah, who sat up as well and started saying, "what, what, where is he? Who is that? What's going on?"

Rose waved her hand at Deborah to wait a minute. "How is he? Did you find out where he is? Did he ask about me? Or my father? What was he like?"

"Well," Marie hesitated. "He was kind of distant, but very sweet. Yeah, he asked about you. Said he hadn't seen you in awhile. He said he was fine, but he was evasive, Rose. I asked him what he was up to and if he was working, and he said he was staying out of trouble and making a living. He was real friendly with this Lucinda Potts, and he seemed to like that baby — her name is Dawn. He said to say hello to you."

"Well, Jesus, Marie, did you get a phone number or some way I can get in touch with him?"

"No, Rose. I asked him, and he said he didn't have a phone. I asked him where he was staying. He said right near where he worked. I asked him where that was. He said Syracuse, like that answered it. I couldn't keep pushing at him. He clearly didn't want to say too much. But he looked okay. Still pretty big, you know, but he said he was fine. I'm sorry I couldn't get any more out of him, Rose, but maybe you could talk to this Lucinda. She seemed pleasant enough."

"I will. Is she at the hospital now?"

"She was when I left. And the baby is going to be discharged tomorrow."

"Okay, I'll go over there now. Thanks a lot, Marie. I'll talk to you later."

Rose hung up the phone. Deborah waited expectantly, watching her to see what she'd do next.

"Well. Sonny showed up at the hospital to visit some baby that was admitted. Sounds like he's friends with her mother. I'm going to go over there. Will you come with me?"

"Of course. I love playing detective. We better take a shower first." She grinned, then kissed Rose. "Who do you want to be, Kojak or Baretta?"

"Baretta. I think he's Italian." She grinned back at Deborah. "But let's hurry up. This is the first real lead we've had."

twenty

IN THE DREAM *someone came to wake him. He was sleeping in a strange room. It was his Aunt Louise, his Momma's sister, and she was tense, the message urgent. "Get up, Sonny, get up now. Come on, brush your teeth. Get ready, she wants to see you." "Who?" he said in the dream, "who wants to see me?" He didn't want to go. A fear awoke in his chest that filled him with dread, with horror. Aunt Louise stood in the doorway, beckoning him with her hand, her eyes blazing, her plump figure a blur to him from his bed in the dream, and he without his glasses on yet. And still, he could see her black eyes blazing, her hand beckoning him, the print of her blue house dress blurred, her black shoes solid on the floor, her legs fixed and still, urging him up, waiting like a guard at the door of this strange room. He didn't want to go; he knew he had to. He reached for his glasses, put them on, and the lenses fell out. Panic rose in him like a late afternoon storm. His mouth grew dry, his stomach tightened, and a flock of twittering birds took flight in his chest. He fixed his glasses, his hands trembling, watching Aunt Louise for a sign of safety she never offered. She just stood there beckoning him with a waving of her hand—faster, faster—till he rose wearing only boxer shorts, their maroon flecks swimming as he looked down at himself. He got up and followed Aunt Louise down*

95

a darkened hallway, its wood paneling seeming to shine as though it'd been rained on, down the hallway till another room opened on his right and Aunt Louise said, "Here, Sonny, she is in here. She has to tell you something." And he looked in and saw only the back of a woman he knew so well and couldn't place, a back straight and strong, the back of a woman standing at the sink doing dishes. He heard the ssshhing sound of the water running, could see the steam rising up over the sink in front of this woman whose face he couldn't see yet, who radiated with the necessity of the message, and the panic again rose in him fierce as thunder. He knew now she had something no one else could tell him. He watched her arms go in and out of the water, saw her shoulders slender and filled with urgency, her hair pulled back into a bun, the blackness of it streaked heavily with an iron gray, and she was about to turn to face him and the dream shifted. He was a little boy, four or five, standing at the top of a winding staircase in the old house, the top of the stairs narrow as a funnel's spout, the light dim as the stairway wound away. Then the bottom where the landlord John Pepe waited with his daughter Geraldine, his friend. She was his friend, and they both looked up at him saying, "C'mon Sonny, c'mon, it's all right," and fear gripped him. He clutched his Momma's hand tight, could feel her presence in this dream like warmth, like safety, his little heart racing toward the danger of the climb down the stairs and his Momma's hand on his shoulder, warm through the white cotton shirt he wore. A faint smell of garlic and soap rose from her hand in the dream, and he leaned into that hand and began to fall   fall   fall down those horrible stairs screaming a horror.

And another move in the dream. Again Aunt Louise, suddenly turning to him with a change of heart, "Maybe not yet, Sonny. You don't have to go to her, you can wait. You can wait awhile." But he raised up his eyes to meet Aunt Louise's,

*and her face turned into John Pepe's face, and he was spiral-
ing downward with the awful sensation of knowing something that terrified him.*

*Aunt Louise is dead. Trouble comes in threes. Never go
with someone who is dead when they call you in a dream.
You will die.*

He woke on Sunday at dawn, drenched with sweat, his
heart throbbing in his throat, his head filled with a blistering
pain knocking against his eyes, the nausea of panic pushing
up in his stomach. And again, now only *trouble comes in
threes.* He couldn't stop hearing that. A yellow pale light
came into his bedroom, and it hurt him, went straight to his
insides where he ached like his guts had taken a beating—his
arms, his legs, all of his skin tender. Even the sheets lying on
him felt wrong. The pounding in his poor head hammered at
him, blurred his vision.

He got out of bed off balance, frightened, and stumbled
into the kitchen for his pills and some aspirin. He was trying
desperately to rid himself of that sensation of horror, of the
terrible thing that scratched at the back of his head just out of
reach. He put the lights on and looked around his rooms for
something that would root him back, something he could see
or touch or smell that would take him back to this Sonny he
was, here, not in the dream that wisped away somewhere just
out of reach.

He went into the bathroom, stood pissing, still groggy, and
saw the mayonnaise jar filled with change on the shelf. Shaking his head to clear it, splashing cold water on his face and
cleaning his glasses, he remembered it was Sunday, and he
could call his Momma. The thought of that entered him, a
warmth, tender to him, and he felt his shoulders relax a little.

He leaned against the sink for the relief of something
sturdy, feeling better, yet still hearing it, the phrase, over and
over: *trouble comes in threes.*

◆

Rose woke up on Sunday, early morning light coming into her bedroom, close against Deborah who slept on. At first Rose couldn't quite place the nervous sensation fluttering in her stomach. She loved Sunday—the papers, coffee in bed. It was one of her and Deborah's favorite times. With a little luck, she could cajole Deb into making an omelet while she lay in bed and did the crossword puzzle, smoking and re-laxed. She savored the thought of spending this day that way and remembered immediately what she would do instead. "Errrr," she groaned into Deborah's back, who responded in her sleep, "What, Rosie, what time is it. What are you moan-ing about?"

"I just remembered what I have to do today. I wish you would come with me."

"I can't Rosie, I don't think it's right. You should see your father yourself." She was talking without waking completely up, turning to Rose, her body warm with sleep. "I'll see you tonight. Anyway, what time is it? We probably have hours before you have to go."

"Yeah. It's seven. I said I'd be there around noon."

"See? Seven o'clock on a Sunday, Rosie. I'm gonna kill you. Go back to sleep. Quit talking to me. Seven o'clock for Christ's sake." And Deborah did go back to sleep, while Rose lay there and brooded for a few more minutes. She got up and put the coffee on, collected the newspaper from the porch, sat smoking in the kitchen waiting for the coffee to brew, and over the first cup tried to rehearse what she was go-ing to tell her father.

When she and Deborah arrived at the hospital yesterday, she met Lucinda Potts and saw the baby Dawn, but Lucinda hadn't given her any information. She was friendly to Rose but kept insisting she didn't know Sonny that well, that she'd just bumped into him coincidentally in the hospital. She said she figured Sonny was visiting someone else. Although she didn't know where he lived or worked, Lucinda said she would tell him to call Rose if she saw him again. Rose gave her her phone number just in case Sonny had lost it, or in case Lucinda ran into him and could let Rose know. She had tried to make light of looking for her brother, telling Lucinda only that she hadn't seen him for awhile, that her father hadn't seen him, and that they were both a little worried about him. "No big deal," she told Lucinda, "we just really want to hear from him."

Rose was sure that Lucinda knew more about Sonny than she was letting on. She smiled to herself, shaking her head, running her hand through her hair as she sat at the kitchen counter drinking coffee. How on earth, she wondered, did Sonny ever hook up with this Lucinda and Dawn Potts? What was their connection? It flitted through Rose's mind that Sonny and Lucinda were lovers, and immediately she dismissed that possibility. Lucinda had been nice enough with Rose, though she was clearly guarded; she was also awfully sweet with her baby. But Lucinda was streetwise, and Rose would forever think of Sonny as almost innocent, if not nearly totally naive.

And what, Rose wondered, to tell her father. He had never been one to stop and think about the things he did, the effects of his habits and moods on his family. He was not a stupid man, though, and he was bound to see eventually that at least a part of Sonny's disappearing act was a reaction to him.

Rose knew that Dominic was governed almost completely by his emotions, that he was a creature of excesses and moodiness. He could no more control the motion of his shifting moods than the ocean could argue with the ideas of the moon: in her father, emotion was an ocean. Sometimes it seemed to her that dual forces of energy surged in him, like a rip tide. He could be irresistible and light-hearted, as he had been with Rose on the telephone. Rose had learned, as each member of the family had, that these upswings were more omen than harbinger, for they were almost always followed by the hours of a moody low tide. Days would pass with her father silent behind a gray wall of suppressed rage, the violence in him crackling like the air before a sudden summer thunderstorm. They'd all moved around him nervously, cautious as cats, knowing that a single wrong word or gesture could charge the current that would short out his nervous system. There was no way to avoid it.

Rose sighed. She could feel the tension in her rising, remembering the way the whole family had navigated the sea in their lives that was father and husband, his volatility omnipresent. His outbursts were too often given to scenes with the belt being ripped from the loops of his pants and raised up over his head in that threatening stance, followed by the whine of leather through air on its downward arc to its target, most often Rose. She had never learned the ruse of passivity, no matter how hard Josephine had tried to drum it into her. Rarely did he strike Lorraine, for even as a baby, Lorraine had worn a sadness in her chocolatey eyes that Dominic seemed to recognize.

With Sonny, though, Dominic's rage took on a different, more insidious form: one of ridicule and the art of humiliation, of emasculation in its purest, most vicious manner, as only male can do to male. Rose had thought about this often, the small and more deep ways her father had tormented Sonny—laughing at his sensitivity; calling him a sissy or a girl; trying, forever trying, to impose on his son that limited social imperative of prescribed maleness. Rose remembered her father's stories about growing up Italian during the Depression and thought she could in some way understand Dominic's need to be so rigid in his definitions. She also thought the time had come for her father to at least begin to re-evaluate those definitions.

But Dominic held still to his ideas of social order, even though those ideas had often been in contradiction to the way he lived his life. Rose knew that although her father never went to church, he swore by the Ten Commandments. He believed that he believed in family, in fidelity, and although he broke his own rules as well as God's with some regularity, he had, all through his reigning tenure as DeMarco patriarch, tried to make his wife and kids adhere to his sense of order. He insisted that girls should wash dishes, that boys should play football. And, while he could make sure that Rose and Lorraine did wash the dishes or scrub the tiles in the bathroom every Saturday morning, nothing he could do would make a football player out of Sonny. Dominic regarded Sonny as a failure, and it seemed to Rose that in some essential way what her father saw as failure in Sonny, he also saw as an even larger failure in himself; he took out all those feelings of his own failure and outrage on his only son.

While Josie was alive, she softened the impact of this on Sonny. When Dominic chastised, insulted, humiliated Sonny, Josie would praise and love and comfort. Rose knew that in her father's eyes, Sonny could do no right, because *he* wasn't right, didn't fit the mold Dominic wanted to cast him in, and for the twenty-six years her brother lived at home, their father had never let him forget it. They were, as the saying goes, between a rock and a hard place. They might as well have been speaking foreign languages to one another, for each spoke the language of his body, and those bodies seemed to have very different systems. Over the years, Sonny grew more fluent in the language of his father, but Dominic, who really believed there was only one language — his, always — never picked up so much as a phrase or a gesture from his son. In fact he never once acknowledged that Sonny was simply being Sonny, that he had no more choice than Dominic had in being Dominic.

Rose drank her coffee slowly, trying to think about how to give her father the latest information. First he hears that Lorraine is living with a Black man, and now the only connection they had to Sonny was through a Black woman. She knew that Dominic would rave and rant about *melanzane;* bad enough, he would say, that Curtis wasn't Italian, but *Black?* And, when he heard about Lucinda, he would probably throw up his hands in that mixture of disgust, utter nonunderstanding, and giving up — none of which he really meant.

Well, Rose thought, he does have a lot to accept: me with Deborah Flynn — and she's not Italian either, she laughed to herself — Lorraine with Curtis Fuller, and now Sonny apparently close to Lucinda Potts. Jesus, I wonder what he's going to think we should do. *I* wonder what we should do. At least we know he's all right.

The last thing she'd said to Lucinda was to give Sonny one other message: "Tell him," Rose had said, "that we all really hope he'll be at St. Vincent's on the twenty-first. It's at nine o'clock. He'll know what I mean."

Rose poured herself another cup of coffee, and one for Deborah as well, and returned to bed until it was time to go.

◆

Dominic sat in the kitchen waiting for Rose. He'd just taken a shower and shaved; the scent of soap and Old Spice surrounded him in the kitchen. Sunday. Jesus but he missed Josie. By now, he thought, the sauce would be on; maybe the kids would be around for dinner, instead of this, sitting like an old man in this kitchen, making my own coffee. And today he was going to make his own sauce. He sat there at the wood-look formica table, glancing around the kitchen. He felt at once the loneliest and the closest to Josie in this room. The things she liked were all around: the God is Love plaque that had to be at least twenty years old; the tiny Infant of Prague statuette on the windowsill over the sink, its red robes slightly dusty; the holy card of St. Lucy he had stuck up on the cork message board soon after the funeral; the collection of porcelain and ceramic birds that Josie had loved and collected through the years. Her latest parakeet, Tweetie Three, had died a couple of months after Josie, but the wicker cage still hung in the kitchen near the refrigerator, its swing and the dangling red and white striped ball toy unmoving in the air of the cage.

When Rose called yesterday and asked to come over, she said she had some information about Sonny. Nothing major, she said, only that she'd run into someone who seemed to know him. Rose hated talking on the phone with him as much as he hated it; it made them both nervous. Well, anyway, Josie, he thought to himself, I told you I'd try to find him. And Rosie is helping me. He took the pork neck bones and chop meat from the refrigerator. Maybe Rosie'd be hungry and, he thought, "I can still make pretty damn good sauce."

◆

He shook his head in confusion. "I don't know Rosie, what's happening lately? Nothing's the way I thought it would be. When I was your age, it was different, it meant something. Family meant something. Marriage, everything was different, Rosie, do you know what I mean? Now? Now it's nothing. Nothing. I got one grandkid I never even see. You, I know about you, Rosie, you'll never have kids, and Sonny, Jesus, what are we doing?"

"Two grandkids, Poppa."

"What do you mean, two...who besides Donna...?" His voice trailed off as he realized what Rose was telling him. "Oh Jesus, perfect, right, of course, now she has another little bastard I'll never see. Probably...Rosie, by the *melanzana?*"

"Poppa, the kid's not a little bastard, he's a sweetheart. You'll love him, and Curtis is okay. I think he's good for Lorraine. She seems happy, Donna looks great. C'mon Poppa, what's the difference, really? She's off drugs completely, and that has something to do with living with Curtis, and with having Junior. You'll see."

"Bull *shit,*" he said emphatically. "I won't see. I don't wanna see. A *melanzana* for Christ's sakes. Is she married at least? What does this guy do?"

"Yeah, Pop, she's married. Curtis works at Crucible. Been there about fifteen years. And they own the trailer."

"Humphh. How'd they do that?" Dominic was fully convinced that even if his kids didn't talk to him, even if they got mad at him and ignored him sometimes, they couldn't really get any place without his help. And, holler and rage as he might, he liked feeling that they needed him to survive. Even angry, he'd rarely refuse them if they asked for help.

"Curtis' family lent them the money for the down payment. It's cute, Poppa. Lorraine has it fixed up real nice. You should see it."

"And how the hell am I supposed to see it when I don't even know where it is? You don't think she'd call me up, say 'how ya doin, Pop,' now do ya? Huh? When's Lorraine ever been nice to me?" His feelings were hurt, not because he hadn't been called, though that did bother him, but because it wasn't he who helped get her set up.

"Pop, you threw her out years ago. Remember?" Rose leaned across the table and touched her father's hand. "Remember? You get too mad sometimes, and you know, Lorraine had her pride too. We all do—even Sonny." She paused. "We get it from you. Look how hard it is for you to call her. Do you think it's any easier for her?"

"Too bad it's not easy for her. I'm her *father.* She should call *me,* out of respect. She has to call me, d'ya understand Rosie? I threw her out because she was going too bad, she was driving your mother crazy. Thank God," he raised up his eyes, "she can't see this now. Lorraine in a trailer with a jigaboo. You, I know with you, Rose, I know about Deborah. Think I'm stupid? And Sonny? Who is this Luisa?"

Rose grinned. "Lucinda, Pop. I don't know. Her daughter was admitted to my floor yesterday, and somehow Sonny knows her, came up to see her baby, Dawn. It may be nothing, I don't know. And Marie Rogers, remember her?" Dominic nodded and Rose continued. "She saw Sonny and said he looked fine. I asked this Lucinda to let him know about the anniversary mass. Marie said she'd call me if Sonny came in today, and Deborah's at my place. She'll get in touch if Marie calls." She stopped. Her father looked suddenly exhausted to her. He sat at the table in a v-neck white tee shirt, the hair on his chest grizzled and white, black pants, brown leather slippers, chainsmoking. His balding head gleamed under the kitchen light. He looked more tired than she thought she had ever seen him, leaning on his hand, his head bent, eyes downcast. She reached out again, touched his face. "It'll be okay. I know nothing's the way you thought it would be, but it will be okay, Poppa. We're all turning out fine, really, even Sonny. This has to be good for him, being on his own. You always said that yourself. His feelings are probably hurt, just like yours are. We're more alike, you know, than we are different. And this is a hard time, Momma's anniversary coming up next week. I know you miss her, Pop."

When Dominic looked up his eyes were filled with tears. "I miss her so much Rosie, I...." His voice broke, and he hesitated. "I know I wasn't perfect, but I loved her. You know that, don't you Rosie? I loved her. She was a saint."

"I know, Poppa. I know. I miss her too. And maybe, just for Momma we can try to work everything out with all of us. You know Momma'd want that before anything else. Right Pop?"

He shook his head again. "Yeah, I guess so. We'll see, Rosie, we'll see."

"Yes, Pop. We will. We'll all see." She got up. No matter how angry, how frustrated she got with her father at times, she loved him deeply. She could see the worry, the hurt in his face; sometimes she thought that for all his *machismo* he was the most vulnerable man she would ever know. She walked around to his side of the table and held him for a minute, feeling her own need to be held just then rise up in her unexpectedly, and had to fight back a sob herself. Dominic let her hug him for a moment, then pulled away and blew his nose. Rose said again, "It'll be okay, Pop. We'll work on it. Now, you sit there and relax. The sauce smells great. I'm going to have a meatball, you want one? Then I'll put the water on to boil. What do you want, fusilli or rigatoni?"

He was feeling better already. He put his glasses on, picked up the newspaper, lit a cigarette. "Fusilli, Rosie, and there's fresh ricotta in the refrigerator. Give me a meatball too."

◆

After eating, they both felt better, as though the meal had given them back something familiar, something they both knew and liked equally, so that any tension between them disappeared in the dishes of fusilli and ricotta. They were having coffee and a cigarette, reading the Sunday paper together at the kitchen table. When the phone rang around two o'clock, they both jumped. "Sit, Poppa," Rose said, "I'll get it." She cleared her throat, picked up the phone. "Hello?"

"Momma?" The voice on the other end of the line was unmistakably Sonny's, hoarse, soft, but Sonny.

Rose felt as though some enormous gulf widened in her chest. Her heart jumped and sped; she hesitated, caught totally off guard.

"Momma?" Again, that voice, sounding slightly desperate. "Sonny?" she finally said, hoping her father wouldn't hear. Now there was a pause on the other end, and she said, "Who is this? Sonny, is it you? Sonny, it's Rosie."

"No," he said "No, I want to talk to Momma."

"Where are you Sonny? You know you can't...Sonny where *are* you...?" She heard the click of the receiver at his end, then nothing.

twenty-one

"YOU KNOW YOU CAN'T...." *Trouble comes in threes. Never go with someone who is dead when they call you in a dream. You will die.* He emerged from the phone booth, wiping the sweat off his forehead, his eyes glazed. He had gotten so hot in that phone booth, but now he felt a coldness begin to tingle at his feet. He stood in the street for a moment, getting colder and feeling the sensation of fear and even a little humiliation, he was not sure why, begin to recede, leaving only a kind of soreness on his skin, the way a bad memory leaves its traces. She had said "you know you can't..." and stopped. She sounded so much like Momma, the fullness of their voices, the way they each said "hello" with the same inflection — kind of rushed, sounding more like "hlo," always as though they were both in a hurry. But it was Rosie, the voice said so, said "Sonny, you know you can't..." and stopped.

He had to be at work by three. There was a dull throbbing in the back of his head, his temples ached. He couldn't remember whether or not he'd taken his pills this morning; he thought he had, but he couldn't be sure. He stood there with his legs wobbling a little, rubbing his eyes. He put his hand inside his coat buttons, through the buttons of his shirt, looking for all the world as though he were about to recite the pledge of allegiance, giving himself something he needed in order to get himself back. The cold ascended up through his groin, his belly. He was calming down. Only the ache now behind his eyes, his vision still murky, his stance uncertain, but he rocked there for a few moments getting his equilibrium slowly in tow, thinking *you know you can't,* until he was finally ready to walk the few blocks to the QuikStar.

◆

"Well, if it isn't Mr. Handsome Pants." Ron's pale blue eyes glinted meanly in the afternoon sunlight. He hadn't fully recovered his cockiness since the night of the fire; he'd left the Star that night feeling demoralized, he wasn't quite sure why, but he didn't like the sensation. Besides, he had to admit to himself that he *had* been a jerk. But what else was he supposed to do? Still, he felt uncomfortable and turned that back on Sonny. Christomighty, he didn't know the guy had fits. "You don't look so good, Sonny."

"Neither do you, Ron. Got anything else to say?" Sonny spoke softly but firmly.

"No." Ron wiped the counter with a gray, damp rag, paused a minute, reached back and untied his apron, eyes cast down the whole time. Then he said, "Oh, yeah. One more thing. *I'll* be back at eleven." He drew his eyes slowly up to look at Sonny.

"What do you mean? Where's Moses?" Even as he asked this question, Sonny felt a prickle of dread at the base of his neck.

"He called about an hour ago. From the hospital. Said he had a coughing spell this morning, went to Emergency. Said they want to keep him a couple three days. He said he'd try to call you here later on."

Sonny felt sick to his stomach. He had an impulse to take off, leave the QuikStar and let Ron get stuck there with his face hanging out, go see Moses. He could do that, he could. He had some money saved up. But something held him back from splitting; he couldn't show what he knew would be seen as another weakness in front of Ron. He'd wait, go see Moses tomorrow, before his appointment with Dr. Rizzo. "What hospital is he in?"

"Upstate, Sonny. The way things are going, you could give that place as your second address."

The only good thing Sonny could see about what had happened was that now he could offer his place to Lucinda, and he could stay at Moses'. Lucinda had said she'd drop in the Star after Dawn was discharged.

Ron left. Sonny had a cup of coffee and tried to think about what to do. Around four, a flurry of customers came in, and it was seven before Sonny knew it. Tonight the special was cheeseburger deluxes and Sonny felt coated with bad grease and the sickening smell of fried, lowgrade beef. Moses still hadn't called, and as soon as he had a chance, Sonny called Upstate and was put through to Moses' room. His voice sounded groggy, filled with a thick sleep. "Moses, it's Sonny. What happened?"

"Oh, Sonny, howya doin? I was gonna call you, but they gave me a shot. I can't seem to stay awake. They wanna keep me here, run some tests. Hell, man, I don't know, you know how they talk."

"Well, listen, I won't keep you awake then. I'll come in tomorrow to see you. But, listen Moses, there's just one thing...."

"What, Sonny?"

"Well, just in case Lucinda can't find a place to stay, you know, because of the fire, I thought I could offer my place, if I can stay in yours. Just for a night or two."

"No problem. You can get the key from Mrs. Boggs, lives up a floor from me. I'm 402, she's 503. She keeps a key for me. Tell her she can call me here if she has any question."

"Thanks, Mo. Listen, ya need anything? Copy of *Hustler* or something to drink? Y'got pajamas?"

"I don't need no pajamas, they got em here. I wouldn't mind some entertainment though." He tried to laugh and got coughing hard again, caught his breath, said, "Okay, well listen Sonny boy, I gotta go. Thanks for calling."

"Sure, Moses. I'll see you tomorrow then." He hung up just as Lucinda was walking through the door, carrying Dawn.

◆

Rose hung up the phone, her palms sweating. The phone call shook her to her roots. Sonny sounded so desperate, asking for Momma. He sounded the way he did when Momma died, asking for her every time he woke up from that deep sleep he'd gone into right around the funeral.

Dominic looked at her over the tops of his reading glasses. "Who was that, Rosie?"

"I don't know, Poppa." She tried to lie, afraid to provoke his temper just now. She was too shaky.

"What the hell ya mean you don't know? Didn't they say who it was? What'd they say, who'd they ask for?"

"Momma."

"*Momma*?" He paused, and seeing the look on Rose's face, his voice, at first incredulous, turned hoarse. He repeated, "Momma? You mean Josie?"

Rose tried to think through the note of alarm in her father's voice. She had to tell him; there was nothing she could do about it. What if it wasn't Sonny? But she knew it had been him, knew that he knew it as well. Did he call on purpose, maybe, to let them know something was off?

"Momma, Pop. It was Sonny."

"Oh, Christ." His reply alarmed Rosie more than Sonny's call had, and that had been considerable: it implied, through the tone in Dominic's voice, that he wasn't all that surprised. "What," he looked at his daughter, "do we do now?"

twenty-two

SONNY WAS NOT quite sure where he was. It was raining, and the small window over near the kitchenette let in a feeble gray light. Already at seven in the morning, the smells of fat and a tired odor of too many bodies seeped into the room. Sonny and his clothes still held the stale reminder of grease; his hair seemed rank with it this morning.

Lucinda had gotten settled in Iris Arms last night. She'd insisted on waiting at the Star so he could take her over there, said she felt weird going into his place without him, at least the first time. At about a quarter to eleven, Sonny'd asked her to wait around the corner, saying he didn't want Ron knowing his business. Lucinda understood, as she always seemed to understand Sonny's need for privacy without asking a whole lot of questions. He didn't tell her about the seizure he'd had the night of the fire. He hoped nobody else — meaning Ron — would tell her either. All this went through his mind as he lay in bed for a few minutes, getting his bearings and trying to shake off the lassitude that seemed to come with the gray morning. He had been pleased with himself last night, arranging for Lucinda and Dawn to stay in his apartment. Mrs. Boggs, a big Black woman, someplace in her sixties he'd guessed, had been a little surprised when he knocked on her door for Moses' key. She hadn't known Moses was in the hospital again, but she gave him the key without much trouble.

Sonny sighed, reached for his glasses, and heaved himself up off Moses' couch. He rummaged around the kitchenette looking for some instant coffee, and put the water in a saucepan to boil on the hotplate before making his way to the bathroom in the hall, coming back in a couple of minutes for a towel. In the shower he thought about his day off: his appointment with Dr. Rizzo was at nine; after that he figured he'd check in on Lucinda and Dawn at his place, and then go see Moses at the hospital. He let the lukewarm water beat on him for a few more minutes, trying to scrub the greasy smell from his hair.

Back in Moses' room he made the instant coffee and sat at the table in the kitchenette. When he looked up, he saw the picture of Moses' mother, or rather, he saw the photograph of a thirtyish Black woman, smiling widely, her dark eyes gleaming. He had, of course, never seen Moses' mother, but he didn't wonder about the picture for a second. He knew who she was; something about the eyes was Moses, something about the way the face radiated a tenderness, a little more guarded maybe on Moses' face, but familiar nonetheless. He wondered what her name was. He knew she was dead, since Moses had told him that much. What did it feel like to have your mother dead, he wondered, as he sat there absently sipping his coffee. *"But Sonny, you know you can't...."* He flashed suddenly on yesterday's call to his Momma and Rosie saying that to him. What did she mean? He still wasn't sure, but as he sat there thinking he felt a sense of dread begin in his belly, and a sudden chill hit him. He looked at his arms: the skin on his forearms was goosebumps, the thick black hairs standing up as if in shock. Outside in the early gray air he could hear the pigeons and the late sparrows peeping frailly through the window. *"Don't forget," the voice said, "don't forget to feed the birds."*

twenty-three

ALL RIGHT, HE ADMITTED to himself, I'm worried. Rose had gone home about an hour after Sonny's phone call, and Dominic's stomach was in an uproar, as were his thoughts. He reached for the Maalox in the refrigerator, trying to settle at least one part of himself. "What the hell," he asked the empty kitchen, "is going on?"

Ever since Sonny had stormed out of the house, Dominic had begun to feel an unpleasant sensation in himself when he thought about him. At first it was just a tiny flutter in the pit of his gut, a sensation like hunger in a recently filled stomach. That had started him on the Maalox, which only helped briefly. Lately, and more and more frequently, thinking of Sonny made him nervous. Josephine hovered in the air over his head. So, was he guilty? Guilt? He started the litany: He's the son, I'm the father, kid's got no respect. Josephine began to evaporate. "Wait!" he cried aloud. He finally had to acknowledge that he was close to panicking. He needed Josie, or the apparition he allowed himself of her, and there was no sense right now in beginning the same old way. Besides, in his heart he knew that Sonny, and the girls too, did respect him, even if they didn't always do what he wanted.

He relaxed a moment, and as he did he saw Sonny's face during that last argument. His eyes had been filled with despair, his face collapsing in what Dominic now could recognize as absolute pain and hopelessness, just before Sonny struck him. Dominic had seen that look only once before. When Sonny had graduated from grammar school, he'd been invited to a pizza party by one of his classmates. With a twinge of — guilt? — Dominic remembered how thrilled Sonny had been by the invite. He'd never mixed much. But it was right after the graduation ceremony, and Dominic had told Sonny he couldn't go, that he had to come to the family party. In a rare act of defiance, Sonny had sneaked off to be with his friends.

Outraged, and embarrassed in front of his brothers, Dominic had stormed into the pizza place and, with a dozen other kids watching, had pulled Sonny by the arm out of the restaurant. In the car, Sonny's face had crumpled into sadness and humiliation, and he had started to cry. This had further enraged Dominic, who began to scream at him for being a sissy, a crybaby, a girl. As they were getting out of the car back at home, Sonny flashed him a look: it was, Dominic realized, the same look he had seen on Sonny's face in the instant before he belted Dominic in the mouth. At that moment, Sonny had finally come of age, and Dominic was just beginning to see it. Ironically, now that Sonny was away from him, Dominic noticed that for the first time he felt real pride in his only son. Right behind that pride, he could finally allow himself to worry.

He considered the possibility that he'd never given Sonny much choice, and that there were ways he might have been pushing him until he would strike out. Still, in some stubborn and ancient sense, he believed that Sonny should come to him, should apologize, for he *was* the father and therefore commanded respect and deference. He was beginning to get a glimmer, if not yet a clear picture, that he had provoked Sonny into leaving so that he wouldn't have to be confronted by what he regarded as a constant reminder of everything that had gone wrong in his life; that he had, in fact, manipulated Sonny to his moment of rage and action.

He sat by himself at the kitchen table, the afternoon turning to dusk, and he felt more alone than he had ever known was possible. A sob threatened his throat, and Dominic wished that just once more he could lay his head on his wife's breast and feel the comfort of her delicate hand brush his cheek.

twenty-four

FOR SONNY, EVERYTHING since that day in April when he'd punched his father in the mouth had taken on new meaning. It was as though he had finally borne himself up and through the life he knew at home. For twenty-four years he survived the ambiguity of his father's feelings for him because of Josie. In the two years since her death, he floundered in a sea of dissonance and fog, never quite finding a way to float without aching deep within himself, though he did not speak of it or think of it consciously. He just lived it, simply felt it as a yellow blur around the edges of everything.

Through this time, Sonny learned something more about withdrawal, about the ease, really, with which he could remove himself from his surroundings. He learned he could pull himself deep into a place in his own center, his own emotion, guided always by a vision of a point of golden light on the inside of his mind that was hope, courage, that finally flashed brighter and more intensely the day of the fight with his father. He had acted for himself in rage, but more important, out of necessity, out of his need for survival, choosing for the first time ever, himself.

Since that day he had been busy recreating his world. Memories had begun to pour in on him—in sleep, in waking, in the middle of conversations with Moses, or while slicing tomatoes or pouring coffee at the QuikStar. He would remember the *feeling* of a moment from the other time, the yellow ache of it, while something else in him now also began to build. He wanted something back, and the thought of his mother was always around him like a slow and patient cloud in the atmosphere of his mind that had changed forever. He was always shaping and reshaping the past, leading himself toward a single inevitable path of action that he thought of as the future, his future, and it included his mother more for what she represented than anything else. But Sonny didn't quite realize that.

In a profound way Josie had become Sonny's guiding saint. Much as Josie prayed to St. Lucy for understanding and light, Sonny offered up countless prayers to his mother, a kind of St. Patience, and he invoked her spirit. As St. Lucy had helped his mother see her life more clearly, more acceptingly, St. Patience led Sonny to the golden kernel of himself. She reminded him that patience is a miracle of spirit, that good things do come to those who wait, and he waited like a solitary rock peering out of the ocean, letting the tides change around him over and over and over again. He knew without ever doubting that time was with him, that waiting was not a thing of boredom and dull hours but a new motion, riveting in its intensity, supreme in its surety. For the first time, Sonny had a purpose; for the first time he was walking through his life without fear.

But something in this morning had made him feel a twinge of alarm: the gooseflesh on his forearms, the flutter of anxiety in his belly, the memory of Rosie's voice the day before. Though Sonny was understanding something about patience from his guiding saint, he was not without his own influence from St. Lucy — some other vision, some other memory was struggling to come to light. Try as he did to keep it in the dimmer recesses of his mind, he could feel it moving out of control in him, moving closer to that kernel of gold. It was intrusive and demanding and tinted with a brilliant, violent red that seeped into his veins till his head throbbed with it.

Time was playing its own trick on Sonny DeMarco. For the past eight months he'd been practicing memory, and those months had keened his ability. Lately, though, he was finding it harder and harder to be selective about what he recalled.

◆

"She *said*," Lucinda repeated, "to tell you that they really hope you'll be at St. Vincent's on the twenty-first. At 9:00 a.m. Said you'd know what she meant. I forgot to tell you Saturday." Lucinda finished packing up Dawn's diaper bag. Adora Delight had already found another apartment, and she and Dawn were going to move in with her for awhile. Sonny sat on the red couch holding the baby who seemed to have fully recovered from her brush with death. He had just come from the doctor's, from the news that Dr. Rizzo wanted to run a couple of tests—a blood test and something called a CAT scan. The office nurse had drawn the blood, but he had to go to the hospital for the other test. Dr. Rizzo made him an appointment for that afternoon at one. Sonny had no idea what the test was; he was nervous about it. His head was throbbing.

"St. Vincent's on the twenty-first," he mumbled, half to himself, in a deadened voice, hearing something like the distant roll of thunder rumbling in the background keeping time with the pounding in his head. "What's today?" He looked over at Lucinda, now sitting on the other end of the couch, smoking a cigarette.

"Monday, Sonny. The sixteenth. Saturday is November twenty-first."

Dawn suddenly began to whimper and fuss. Lucinda, reaching for her, looked at Sonny. "Are you all right?" His face had gone chalky white, his eyes flat. When he didn't answer right away, she poked his shoulder. "Hey, Sonny," she said, a note of confusion in her voice, "you all right? You're scaring Dawn."

He shook his head, took off his glasses, and rubbed his aching eyes. "Huh?" He shook his head again, replaced his glasses, looked at Lucinda, forcing himself to focus, to shake the blurriness away. Then he touched his chest through the buttons on his shirt. *Something fluttered in the air around him, the hands of someone who was clearly dying, paper dry, their fluttery motions all askew, searching. He could feel their dryness tugging, pulling, an urgency in their motion, the tiny veins on the hands like a roadmap of memory or horror. Inside his shirt now touching his chest, beseeching him to remember something, and he felt more than heard a sound like water on a lit match hiss in his chest near where his heart lay, fragile and tender as a white bird aching to be freed, its frail peeping like a distant lament.*

Lucinda poked him again. "Hey, Sonny, wake up. Where you at?" She stopped, struck by the look on Sonny's face—a look of horror, the corners of his mouth beginning to twitch. In the next second she realized he was crying. Without thinking, holding Dawn with one arm against her hip, she reached out with her free hand and touched Sonny's face, and the touch broke through something in him. A sob burst from his throat, and he, also for once without thinking, gave into a need so huge in him to be held, buried his face against Lucinda's chest and cried for what he still could find no words for.

twenty-five

SONNY WOKE FROM a mean sleep. He woke and rose, lumbering and groggy. Right behind his right eye, almost inside his right eye, was a pounding, a throbbing dense and thick and persistent. All of his body felt sluggish, like his blood was moving wrong, or not moving at all, like it was inside him and needed to scream or run but everything was fixed, immobile. It was the blood of rage, a rage so deep and so old that every cell and every corpuscle throbbed. His right eye pounded, the eyelid twitched, and in his mean and tormented sleep he had seen the nightmare vision, had heard its profound rumbling like an angry sea, like the earth finally rearing up its outrage—mountains crumbling, the ground splitting, the grimace of trees against a purple sky.

Through it all a single gold beacon was visible deep within his mind, urging him up, past the pounding and roaring of that unnameable rage, past his resignation to it as his lot. Now that gold light drew him further and further inside himself till the pounding over his right eye seemed so removed from him that he could feel it as someone else's pain. Finally all he saw was that gold blazing like the thing he'd always needed, and he followed it. He needed it, needed to feel something warm on the inside of his own skin. He rose and swayed still groggy, still naked, without his glasses, and tried to push through his own memory to the dream which was not a dream but a nightmare—all tangled and full of reeds and swamp grass and the damp swell of weeping.

The blue envelope in the dream with a spidery name across the top, Josephine. He peered at it, in his dream without glasses, he peered till he could make it out: Josephine. And like a reverberation he heard it again and again—Josephine Josephine Josephine—and the name on the envelope swelled and moved, the letters like live things now screaming Josephine, and he took the envelope and opened it. Inside a holy card, St. Lucy holding a dish, the dish holding a pair of eyes, eyes Sonny had to squint in the dream to see. The dish, St. Lucy's eyes, his Momma's name on the envelope, the envelope a pale, pale blue, the handwriting spidery but clearly Josephine, Josephine. He looked at the envelope, at the holy card again, St. Lucy holding her own eyes on a plate. He wanted to turn the card over, see the prayer. He read, in his dream he read what was on the back of the card.

> *Love Conquers All*
>
> *How sweet the cross! How painless falls the steel!*
> *Are these pangs all that of death I feel?*
> *A thousandfold such wounds my love shall heal.*
> *Love carries me through all, love conquers pain;*
> *O let me die indeed, but die without a stain.*

Sonny tried to see what else, who the card was for, why this holy card in his dream with his mother's name on the envelope. He saw a date, November twenty-first, on the back of the card. He saw it, and in the dream his head began to pound. He felt his eyes, his right eye pulsing, saw his own eye red in the dream, red as blood and as full of rage, and all he knew was his eye'd gone red. He couldn't read any more—the card, the date, the picture of St. Lucy all blurred—just Jose-

phine, the sound whispered along his spine, Josephine, Jose-phine.

And he woke in darkness and naked, unsure of the time or the day or of anything but his eye pounding, and then the light, and he stood near swooning in the dark and groggy room till he leaned way back into himself, into the light he saw, golden as the chalice at mass that last time in November. He saw it golden, shining and round, and he followed it, falling back onto the bed into sleep.

◆

His day off had exhausted him. He felt as though all of it had been spent chasing after something that kept eluding him, and he was drained. Not only had he had to be more places in one day than was usual for him, but he felt invaded, exposed: the blood test at Dr. Rizzo's, the raw emotion that poured from him when he cried in front of Lucinda, and the CAT scan—the sense he had the whole time the test was in progress that something was wrong, that he was letting himself in for trouble going through with it. Yet he felt trapped, as though he had no choice; it would have raised too many questions with Dr. Rizzo if he had balked. Rizzo had been the DeMarco family doctor for as long as Sonny could remember and knew them all. Sonny had a recollection of him from long ago, after the time Lorraine had been brought home drunk, the night Dominic beat her. That same night he also demanded that Joe Rizzo come out to the house and examine her, find out if she'd been fucked. After the doctor saw her and Dominic had receded into gloominess, slinking off to the parlor to brood, Dr. Rizzo came into the kitchen where a young Sonny sat with his mother and Rosie. Each of them was on edge, afraid to speak above a whisper, knowing anything could and probably would set Dominic off again. He looked at them in the dim light of the kitchen and put an arm around Rose, saying simply, "Your father is a very difficult man."

Sonny remembered this, for it was the first time anyone outside the immediate family had acknowledged the difficulty of living with Dominic. It was also the first time it occurred to Sonny that not everyone lived this way; if the doctor saw Dominic's behavior as "difficult," then it must have been uncommon. Sonny had felt a surge of relief at the realization, and he had seen the relief also on the faces of his mother and sister.

Joe Rizzo knew them too well for Sonny to be able to refuse the CAT scan. He would probably have called Rose at the hospital to talk with Sonny, and that would raise more problems than going through with the test itself. So he had gone. Afterwards he went to see Moses and was horrified to find him looking gaunt and yellowish, and so listless; even the flask Sonny sneaked him didn't light up his eyes. Moses had just lain there, arms loose at his sides, the white hospital johnny coat seeming to accent his sickly pallor and label his hopelessness.

By the time Sonny got back to Iris Arms he was worn out. He fell into a deep sleep almost as soon as he hit the couch, and woke only once before morning—with the dream, the nightmare, the light of it screaming against his eyes. His eye pounded relentlessly, and though he woke and stood and tried to clear his mind of it, and then fell back to sleep, in the morning he woke again without yet remembering what it was he had relearned in the night.

twenty-six

ROSE WAS GLAD that this looked like a slow day on pediatrics. She'd stayed up late the night before printing the shots of Lorraine and Curtis and the kids. The night nurse had just finished giving report, and while the staff was busy with breakfast trays, pre-ops, and early treatments, Rose made out the day's assignments over a cup of coffee in the nurses' station.

She was not terribly surprised when she looked up and saw Joe Rizzo emerge from the elevator and head toward her desk. She scanned the charts again to see if he had a patient on the floor. He didn't, but every now and then he stopped up just to say hello, see how the family was doing. He'd been the family doctor since Rose was a kid, and ever since the night that Dominic had beaten Lorraine and called Joe Rizzo to the house to examine her, Rose held a particular fondness for the doctor. That night — almost twenty years ago now, yet Rose never saw him without the memory resurfacing — he'd seen Dominic's temper in full force, seen the welts from the strap on Lorraine's back and thighs. As Dominic brooded in the parlor while his wife and kids sat silent and terrorized in the kitchen, Joe Rizzo had come into the kitchen and stood quietly, his presence comforting. Rose could recall that moment with absolute clarity: the dark kitchen, the eerie silence, the dim light and tension. In the aftermath of the familial violence and struggle that had seemed to leave the atmosphere dense and yet fragile, frightened but hopeful, there was an ironical hope in the release of tension that action, even violent action, brought with it. And Joe Rizzo had stood, just a little outside the circle of table and family, had looked at them all and put his arm around Rose and said simply, "Your father is a difficult man." That simple statement had, in its own way, released Rose from pretense. She remembered him the way she remembered the young curate at St. Vincent's, Father Michael, whom she could talk to outside of the confessional, for both of them had come into her life at about the same time, and each had given her courage and a desire for change.

Now she watched Joe Rizzo approach her desk. He's getting old, she thought. He limped just slightly, the only visible effect of the mild stroke he'd had the year before. Just now his bushy salt and pepper eyebrows were drawn together, his eyes downcast, hands stuffed in the pockets of the white lab coat he wore.

Rose got up from her chair, leaving the assignments for the moment. "Good morning," she said, and walked around the nurses' station, kissing him on the cheek. "What brings you up here so early?"

"Hello, Rose." He took her hand in his own. "Do you have time for coffee? I have to talk with you, about Sonny. It's important." He spoke quietly, his voice somber.

"Is he all right?" A little alarm went off in her. She felt as though she had known this was going to happen and somehow was prepared, vividly remembering her father's tone of voice after Sonny called on Sunday.

"I hope so Rose. I saw him yesterday, did blood levels, an EEG, and sent him for a CAT scan. He seemed okay then, but the radiologist called me this morning. There's an AV malformation, Rosie. We've got to find him. I want to talk with you before I call the house and talk to Sonny. Can you leave the floor?"

"Yes, it's slow. Let me catch up with Marie, and then I can leave."

◆

"So," the doctor pushed away his coffee cup. "We have to get in touch with him right away." He glanced at his watch; it was 9:00 a.m. "Will he be at work now? Do you have the number there?"

A dull heaviness had settled in Rose's chest. Sonny was, even right at this moment, in danger. And she had no idea how to find him. It was clear that Joe Rizzo was totally unaware of the family situation. "Joe," Rose could hear the quiet horror in her own voice, "he hasn't lived home since last April. He had a fight with my father. I have no idea where he is."

Joe Rizzo shook his head slowly; he was hardly surprised, but even more concerned. He looked up at Rose. "Some things," he said quietly, "never really change, do they Rose?"

She explained to him as best she could. Then she went up to the floor, told Marie she was in charge, that she had to find Sonny—it was an emergency. She pulled the discharge chart on Dawn Potts, took the address and phone numbers from it, and left the hospital, filled with a sense of dread and purpose.

◆

What Rose learned from Dr. Rizzo was alarming; most horrifying was the fact that at any moment Sonny's brain could literally explode on itself. He was like a walking time bomb. The problem revealed by the CAT scan showed that clearly, and Sonny had probably had it since birth—an arterial-venous malformation in his temporal lobe, a vessel weakness that could give way any time.

As Rose listened to the doctor, things began to fall into place. This had been with Sonny all his life but had gone undiagnosed until the CAT scanning technique became available. It was complicated by the seizure disorder and the early hydrocephaly that Sonny was also victim to. Joe Rizzo thought that Sonny must have had a small hemorrhage when Josie died. That would explain the headache, the nausea, the severe lethargy and confusion. Somehow the bleeding had tamponaded itself relatively quickly, limiting its damage. And the temporal lobe, where the vessel weakness lived — covert and lethal and patient — was the storehouse of memory. It was also home of the parts of the hypothalamus that affect the limbic system, involved in motivation and emotion, and intimately related to memory.

Rose took in this information with a growing sense of fear and a gnawing sensation of guilt. For the first time she was glad her mother was not alive, was relieved that she wouldn't have to explain this to her, for in Joe Rizzo's explanation of Sonny's medical problems was confirmation of Sonny's difference. Rose wondered at what point Sonny's body had started to rebel on itself. She believed firmly that Sonny had been marked long before his birth and thought again of the small cross on Sonny's forehead. Yes, it was more stigma than scapular. Yes, it had been a sign that set him apart, gave witness to the cross he had to bear throughout his lifetime — a cross weighted first by emotional difference and then by his body in its own response to what was real, taking on the distortion and disease that had been foisted upon it.

The interconnectedness of spirit and body, the intimacy with which the body responded to the thwarting of the spirit, altering itself finally into the grotesque — systems askew, searching always for reorganization, the possibility of harmony—seemed clear to Rose. Sonny had never been permitted to follow or praised for following his true nature, had never been allowed to express the gentleness, the sweetness that had also marked him since birth. Instead, he was ridiculed by Dominic, persistently, cruelly, always hounded to be what he was not.

What, Rose wondered, would Sonny have been like if he had been born female, or wealthy, been allowed to grow into himself rather than the way he had been made to feel: implicit in every motion, every emotion, was that something was wrong. He was always at odd and sharp angles, knocking up against what was expected of him. Never did the mirror reflect himself the way he saw himself—from the inside; no, always he was reminded of the disparate images. Rose remembered with a sense of acute poignancy how he had watched their father dress. How, as he grew to adolescence, he tried to mimic his father's walk, a swagger really, that *was* Dominic, but never, never would be Sonny. yet, how he had tried, and repeatedly failed.

In a curious way, it was Sonny's weight that finally began to give him a sense of who he was. He was about sixteen when he started to get heavier and heavier. This, after years of being scrawny, of not eating well, of pleas and coaxing and demands to eat as a younger boy. He had, the older he got, begun to eat more and more, to alter, for all the world to see, his body: to become in size and shape as different from his father as possible. The weight gave Dominic yet another reason to berate him, but in this one Sonny was in control. He and only he decided whether or not to eat, and just as throwing his dinners behind the couch in the parlor as a little kid had been an attempt to control his life, the overeating took on the same importance. With it came a silence, an immutability that increased and grew intractable. He lived an existence that often looked inert as a snail's, but had in com-

mon with the snail nothing but the hard exterior protecting its
soft inner self.

As Rose walked from the hospital into the damp November
air she was almost entranced by the recognition she felt in Dr.
Rizzo's explanation: he had confirmed what was already
quite clear to her. Realizing that left her responsible for what
she had known and ignored. She had chosen to watch Sonny
grope and dangle at the end of what turned out to be a very
short line, rationalizing her acceptance of his pain by her own
need to carve out her life, separate from the family, as different from the way she grew up as she could imagine. She
had done it twice, she could see that, first with Lorraine and
then with her brother. Even now, as she drove toward her father's house, the sky marbled in grays and a pale yellow, the
threat of rain or wet snow ominous, she could understand all
the intellectual reasons why she had had to move away from
her family, why she'd picked the path she did to survive. Lorraine and Sonny had done the same thing, only done it differently; and she knew she should have taken what she learned
in the larger world and used that knowledge to at least *see* her
sister and brother for who they were. She was getting that
chance with Lorraine. She hoped she would have it with
Sonny.

The colors of the sky were a reflection of the color of the
mood Rose was in, her navy blue Toyota speeding down
Route 81 to North Syracuse, still in her white uniform, thinking of that day in July at the cemetery when she had promised
her mother she would look for Sonny soon. She saw betrayal
heaped upon betrayal this threatening morning, and she
drove on, driven by the desire she hoped was not too late in
coming, to try and set things right. She was going home.

twenty-seven

SONNY WAS SLOW WAKING UP. His head had begun to ache, the familiar throbbing dense behind his eyes, and something new was happening. There was a fleeting and burning sensation in his right temple that fanned out just over his eye, a sudden jolt of pain that stilled him when it hit. With it came a plan, an old plan, the one he had abandoned the day he'd gone Christmas shopping with Lucinda. That day seemed long ago now to Sonny. He remembered it as though it were in some odd way the future, or as though he were looking into one of those snow-filled glass balls in which he could dimly see himself on the bus and at the shopping center with Lucinda and Dawn. He could see it vaguely, but he could recapture none of the warmth he had felt holding Dawn against his chest that day. Thinking of it now his lip drew up into a kind of snarl, an expression of intense self-mockery, the expression he was sure Lucinda would wear if she were here.

The pain in his head threw him off balance. He moved slowly through his apartment, reaching for his pills, checking the calendar—November 17th, Tuesday—the time. He was sure of its importance, and as the hands of the clock moved toward late morning, he knew he wouldn't go to work today, would do none of the things he was supposed to do, and the sneer on his face gave way to a look of cunning. His eyes were drawn close together, his full lips compressed in the convic-

tion of the newly emerging day's plan. The moment he saw it
he began to feel a cold calm settle in him, a chill that mim-
icked the weather's moodiness. He sat for a few more
moments at the kitchen table in his apartment, slowly drinking his coffee, stroking the stubble on his chin, the day
unreeling before his eyes as though it were a familiar movie.
The image was projected in color on the dingy wall he stared
at, dreamlike: the woman standing at a sink doing dishes, her
back only visible to him, the gray-black hair, the white blouse
and apron, and steam softening the picture.

He left the apartment without shaving, without showering,
still in the clothes he had slept in, his dungarees and green
sweatshirt rumpled and smelly. Throwing on his tweed winter
coat with the fake fur collar, ignoring his overshoes, he
moved steadily, but without haste or urgency. He ignored or
pushed any sensation that remained from the dream of the
night before far back into the recesses of his mind, into that
snowy ball where he had Lucinda and Dawn, and now his
eyes were riveted on the images he had seen on the wall. Sonny was pulled along by the desire for one thing and one thing
only: he had to see his mother. He had told Moses once that
forever could change, and he was determined to see that
change, to change it himself if he had to.

He rummaged through his drawers before he left the
house, searching for one of the few objects he'd brought with
him when he left home. On his twelfth birthday, Lorraine
had given him a fishing knife. He found it, the stainless steel
cold and shiny. He extended the blade, still razor sharp, and
with a purpose he did not quite understand and did not trouble about, refolded the blade and slipped it into the pocket of
his overcoat. Sonny kept his right hand curled around it as he
walked outside, his left hand free in the damp and charged
air, gazing at the sky, smelling the dampness in the steely
cold.

He felt his head begin to clear; the throbbing behind his eyes continued, but now it seemed the beat he moved to. Twice on the way downtown he stopped suddenly, a look of pain and confusion, then anger, darkening his features, clamping his eyes suddenly shut. When those red pains stopped, he moved faster, even more certain of this journey. Sonny had to see his Momma. He was going home.

Today he would take no chances with buses, with the slender possibility of seeing anyone he knew. He walked slowly and purposefully the long blocks downtown, intentionally taking his time, for he wanted it to be late afternoon, dusk, before he arrived at the house.

Once downtown, he stood in front of Dey's for awhile, watching people move through the streets, clutching packages or briefcases. A fine rain was falling, the traffic hissing on the slick streets, blending with the constant dull pounding in his head. Something about the grayness of everything struck him deeply, touching off an awful sadness, a sensation like pure grief. All the motion and sound of the streets swirled around him, blurring slightly through his steamy glasses and the throbbing ache behind his eyes. He felt awash in it all — invisible, alone, yet conspicuous and out of place. He could feel his heart ache in the bowl of his chest and yearned for some light, golden and warm, to soothe him. It was only love that Sonny sought, a place to rest. A place he would know safety, a place where his heart could open itself and be wanted. His throat grew tight, and his eyes were suddenly swimming with tears, hot and unexpected, pushing him further into himself. He hated that this was surfacing here, glad only for the rain that mixed with his tears.

Anger surged in him at his vulnerability as he stood, his fingers now curling with their own desire for action around the cold steel in his pocket. He thought of nothing, only ached for what was most familiar, his eyes ablaze with the desperate need for it: Moses and Ron, Lucinda, Dawn, the QuikStar, and Iris Arms all faded, like stories from someone else's life. Jumbled pictures filled his mind as he stood there, bits and pieces of memories or dreams, he could no longer tell the difference: a sparrow tweeted from somewhere, and he saw the yellow canary. Aunt Louise beckoned, a baby against his chest, a man dying in a hospital bed—nothing was connecting, making sense. And then the image of St. Lucy, the plate with her own eyes in her hand, the holy card, the date, and a horror released itself in him. He almost lost his balance, leaned against the wall for a second, shaking his head, confused and growing angrier, a terror raw and violent mixed with the rage boiling in him. Sonny shook his head, touched his own forehead in a gesture of unmistakable tenderness, and hesitating just another minute, walked to the curb and hailed the first cab that came his way.

twenty-eight

OUT AT VALLEY VIEW Trailer Park, Lorraine had just finished cleaning the breakfast dishes. Junior sat on the floor in the living room, happily scribbling with crayons on a huge pad of manilla paper. She flicked on the radio and Kenny Rogers was singing "Don't Fall in Love with a Dreamer." Lorraine poured herself a last cup of coffee and stood for a minute at the kitchen window watching the fine, cold rain fall on the bare trees. Since Rose's visit the past weekend, she'd been moody, not quite depressed, but she felt a nagging, unpleasant sensation, almost like homesickness or nostalgia for something she never had. And she couldn't get Sonny off her mind. Last night she dreamed that she and Curtis took Sonny with them fishing up north. In the dream, Sonny sat between her and Curtis in a big rowboat, silent and rocking on the waters of Lake Ontario. It was the rocking that woke her with a sad shift in motion. The dream, or more—the emotion of Sonny in the dream—hung about her like a cloud, and the day's weather accented her melancholy.

She thought of calling Rosie to see if she had any news from Sonny. Lorraine glanced at the clock: it was 11:00 a.m., Tuesday. Rose was most likely at work, and she didn't want to bother her there. Nothing was wrong, nothing was different, or she was sure Rose would have called her. But she couldn't shake the blues or her sense of uneasiness. There was a scratching at the door. Bingo the cat wanted in; he'd been out all night. When Lorraine opened the door, there he stood, his black fur matted with the rain, and dangling from between his teeth was a gray and lifeless bird, its puny little head hanging askew.

Lorraine slammed the door in horror, then stopped herself. What was she doing? Bingo was always bringing trophies home. We live in the country, she reminded herself. But she didn't like it, it gave her the creeps, and instinctively she glanced over at Junior who colored on, quiet and content, seemingly oblivious to his mother's nerves.

She sat at the table, ignoring for the moment Bingo's mewing at the door. Something was going on, she was sure of it. Every sense told her that she was right: something was wrong with Sonny. Yet she wondered, thinking it was just the fact that Momma's anniversary was coming up made her feel a little spooked. Maybe she had been wrong to make so light of Sonny's being gone from home for the last eight months. But, Jeez, she thought, I haven't seen him hardly at all the last few years, so why all of a sudden am I worrying? She wondered if she'd be so worried if she hadn't seen Rose. Although she knew that Rose got her thinking about her brother, the dream last night and the morning's ominousness had nothing to do with Rose's visit.

She wished Curtis was home so she could talk with him about it. "What do you think, Junior?" He looked up at her and grinned, rooting her back home. She grinned back at him, then said, "You think maybe I should call your grandpa?"

Junior's eyes danced, and he repeated delightedly, "granpa, granpa." He was thinking of Curtis' father, but it made no difference to Lorraine. That did it. The hell with these years of silence. Sonny was her only brother, and whether or not her father was pleasant to her, she had to try to find out what was going on.

She lit another cigarette, then picked up the phone and dialed her home number. She was hardly surprised when Rose answered the phone, though her hands began to tremble. "Rosie," she said, "what's going on?"

"Oh, Jesus, Lorraine, I was just going to call you." Rose replied as though she had been expecting the call. "We have to find Sonny, Lor...he's very sick. Can you get out here? I'll explain the whole thing to you when I see you. Do you have the car?"

"No, shit, Curtis kept it today. I didn't feel like taking him to work. I'll see if I can get one of the neighbors to take me, or I'll call a cab. I'll be there as soon as I can." She paused. "Oh, listen Rosie, I'm bringing Junior. Did you tell Pop?" Lorraine was taken aback by the anxiety she suddenly felt about bringing Junior home.

"I told him Lorraine. He was a little uppity about it at first, you know Pop, but now, to tell you the truth Lorraine, I don't think he'll say anything. Listen, get here as soon as you can. I want to keep the phone clear in case we hear something."

"All right, Rose, I'm on my way. And Rosie, take it easy. You're not alone in this one, you know." She hung up and immediately dialed her neighbor, Bernice Rutkowski, who agreed to drive Lorraine into North Syracuse.

Hurriedly now, she bundled Junior, taking a minute to pack a diaper bag for him. She left a note for Curtis and told him to meet her at her father's when he got off work. She threw on a clean shirt over her jeans, ran a comb through her long dark brown hair, and when Bernice honked, she and Junior were ready to roll.

twenty-nine

HER BODY FELT EXHAUSTED, as though she had just completed hours of strenuous exercise. Still in her uniform, she emerged from the house physically spent; yet her mind was fixed on what she now had to do. Rose had explained what Dr. Rizzo told her to Dominic, who wouldn't be persuaded to wait for Lorraine to arrive so that she would only have to repeat it once. He had to know as soon as she walked in the door. She told him of the danger of the AV malformation to Sonny, watching how his face sagged, then creased for a moment with anger. Rose was perplexed at the focus of that anger. She wasn't sure at first whether it was directed toward the sickness, or toward Sonny for having it and causing this upheaval. Then she realized it was both of those things. Anger had moved through her father's face like a shifting cloud. She swore that it changed him completely and knew she would never see Dominic the same way again. Right past the anger came a poignant look of helplessness and need and fear. Rose knew he had wanted to disbelieve what he was hearing, had been going to try to dismiss it gruffly, stubbornly, but found in the fleeting angry moment that he believed it, and more, had somehow *known* it, and was horrified.

And then Lorraine had walked in with Junior, just opened the front door like she was coming home from the grocery store and stood in the doorway for a minute. Junior, in her arms, had brought a finger up to his mouth instinctively, as though he was pondering the situation. The gray light of the day seeped into the house, framing both of them. Rose and Dominic were sitting at the kitchen table, silent, till all four pairs of eyes met midway between the kitchen and the living room, someplace just over the counter dividing the rooms, past the wall where the bulletin board hung with its holy card of St. Lucy. Those four pairs of dark brown and similar eyes lingered for the briefest second in recognition familiar as daily breath, linked eternally through blood and history and love.

Dominic had been prepared to cold-shoulder Lorraine, to ignore Junior, saying to himself that he was just letting them enter his house because of Sonny, but that had been before — even just minutes before. Now when he looked up and swore he could see Josie in the kid's eyes, saw Lorraine slightly fearful of him at the door, Rose poised tense as a bird beside him ready for anything to happen, he could feel nothing but love and kinship. He saw how they were all together minus one, that they were family, together in need and crisis, and that the crises had shifted from one to the other over their lifetimes. In a corner of his mind he could see Josie, serene, nodding her grayed head ever so slightly, and her mouth in not quite a smile (although it looked to him as though a little one was beginning at its corners), but not so much a smile as an expression of knowledge and contentment, radiating with love.

He knew with his skin shivering that love was what he felt, had always felt, and yet he'd ignored its beautiful power. It had been there and was in motion now, tender and delicate and astonishing as a flock of Canadian geese taking flight in unison over the lake, ready to head home. Dominic sat there in a tee shirt and baggy boxer shorts, unshaven, with slow, slow tears gathering in his eyes. He sat there and opened his arms in a gesture filled with the truth of what he was feeling, and Lorraine, still holding Junior, came into them from across the room. With one arm he clasped them to his chest, and with the other he reached over and pulled Rose, too, into the circle that was finally almost complete.

◆

"Just a little luck, just a little," Rose said this to herself as she pulled up in front of the address she found on Lucinda Potts' chart: 28 North Colvin, the number that was over the broken metal mailboxes of the building she was in front of. She squinted up at the house. The windows on the first and second floors had been broken, probably from fighting the fire, and behind them she could see only darkness. A sofa sat on the porch, stuffing spilling from its charred and blackened upholstery. Her heart sank. She knew no one was going to be here, but she determinedly got out of the car anyway, smelling the acrid remains of the fire the minute she hit the air, pulling her down jacket closer to her body more out of a feeling of futility than cold. She walked up to the porch, peered through the ground floor window. Nothing but water-soaked furniture and old newspapers were visible to her. She checked the mailbox, hoping against hope that she'd find some clue to Lucinda Potts' whereabouts.

"You from the Health Department?"

Behind her, so close behind her that she could feel breath on the back of her neck, Rose heard the voice and jumped a mile. She turned quickly.

Adora Delight, in a red leather coat, black tight pants, her hair elaborately plaited, stood, one hand on her hip, her head tilted to the side. She did not like one bit the sight of Rose standing on her porch, burned out or not, and looking through her mailbox like she had some right to. She repeated, "You from the Health Department?"

Adora could not know that the sight of anyone just then on the porch gave Rose a wild surge of hope, and having expected to see no one, she was practically ready to embrace the strange woman, hostile as she was or not. "No," she answered, "no, my name is Rose DeMarco. I...I met Lucinda Potts...no, what I mean is, when Dawn...do you know them—Dawn and Lucinda?" Rose was shaken and couldn't get her thoughts together quickly enough. She had an impulse to blurt out the whole story right away, then realized it was entirely possible that none of it would mean a thing to this woman, who clearly did not like the sight of her there.

"Why do you want to know?" Adora had figured out by now that Rose was not up to harm or interested in snooping. She was entirely too nervous, decidedly uncool, not like the social workers or do-gooders came around when you didn't want them. Still, she didn't know *what* she wanted, and Adora was not going to give away *any* information about anybody till she knew.

"Look," Rose was calmer, "my name is Rose DeMarco. I'm looking for my brother, his name is Sonny. I work at Upstate, on the children's floor. I met Lucinda when her baby was a patient there. Just this past weekend. And she knows Sonny. Do you know where she is?"

"Well, what you want this Sonny for?" Adora hadn't moved, just stood there, not helping Rose out one bit, still not sure what she wanted, or how Lucinda fit in.

"Look," Rose started again, "Sonny is my brother, and I have to find him. I just found out that there's something very wrong with him. He's really sick, but he doesn't know it. I just found out myself." She stopped, trying to impress this woman with the gravity of the situation. "Please," she said, her voice close to breaking. "Please, I don't know where he is, and I'm hoping that Lucinda can help me find him. Please, Miss...." She paused again.

"Delight." Adora relaxed her stance. Rose's urgency broke through her guard. "Adora Delight. You call me Adora. I'm Lucinda's roommate. That your car?" She pointed toward the Toyota.

Rose nodded, and Adora said, "Okay, then, let's go. It's not far from here." She started down the steps, then remembering why she had come in the first place, stopped, turned to Rose, and almost grinning, said, "Did we get any mail?"

◆

At first, Lucinda was as wary of Rose as Adora had been, despite the fact that she had already met Rose and knew she was Sonny's sister. Sonny had been so secretive about her, and Lucinda didn't want to get him in any kind of trouble. She said that to Rose, and Rose replied, for what seemed like the hundredth time, that Sonny was right now, right at this very minute, already in trouble. "He's sick, Lucinda. Real sick. Like he could die at any moment or collapse someplace. I don't know what he's told you about me or the rest of the family, and at this minute I don't much care, but you have to believe me. I'll get the doctor on the phone if you want me to, but if you have any idea where he is, *please* tell me."

Lucinda sat in the new apartment, surrounded by boxes, holding Dawn. She believed Rose. She knew herself that something wasn't right with Sonny. Ron had told her about the seizure, and it was just yesterday that Sonny had broken down and cried. "All right," she finally said, slowly, "all right, Rose, I believe you. I saw him yesterday, and I haven't seen him since."

"Well, where did you see him?"

"At his apartment. It's in Iris Arms. Number 7." She looked at the clock; it was almost one. "He has to be at work at three. At the QuikStar, the one downtown. Or you could try Moses. Sonny could be visiting him."

"All right. Who's Moses? Where does he live?" Rose was checking off the two places. Iris Arms — Jesus, she thought, so close to where she traveled, and the QuikStar, my God, how could I have missed him? Suddenly she was thinking again of that day at the cemetery, the promise she'd made her mother. I'll make it right Momma, I swear I will.

"Well," Lucinda was saying, "he *lives* in the Clinton Hotel, but he's not there now. He's in the hospital, your hospital. His last name is O'Toole, Moses O'Toole. If Sonny isn't at home or work, he might be with Moses, or maybe Moses'd know."

Rose got up. "All right. Thanks a lot, Lucinda." She fished a pen from her pocket, tore off the top of a matchbook, quickly writing. "And if you see him, please call this number. My father's house. Okay?" She handed Lucinda the match book cover.

Lucinda took it and wrote out her number for Rose. "Would you let me know when you find him? Please? He's a sweet guy, Sonny — your brother. You know?"

"I know." Again Rose found herself suddenly close to tears and coughed trying to hide it. But Lucinda saw. She reached and took Rose's hand, squeezing it slightly. Rose promised to let Lucinda know and headed one more time to the car.

She drove directly from Lucinda's in the direction of Iris Arms, cursing the midday city traffic and her rotten luck on this search. She was getting every red light, seemed to be constantly behind some timid driver who stopped or slowed even before the green light turned amber. Memories, images of her family and especially of Sonny, were floating through her mind, each accompanied by an emotional tug. Twinges of guilt kept surfacing, as well as that sickening wrench in her gut that felt like a blend of guilt and shame. It was such a familiar sensation when she thought about her family. On top of whatever she was feeling now was the sense of urgency, of mission. Though she moved slowly in the traffic, she was speedy, intensely focused, her whole self geared toward finding her brother.

She felt like a detective and remembered the board game she and Sonny and Lorraine used to play as kids, *Clue.* A sound escaped from her lips; it was almost a chuckle. Only the irony made it something else, for it was clear that no one would win this game until all the clues were shared. How Sonny had loved *Clue,* his skinny, little-boy face puckering furiously over each card he drew, delighting in the mystery and secrecy of the game's plots. "Oh, Sonny," she said aloud, "what a time to try and win." For she knew he was fighting for himself now, that what he needed and wanted to win was only himself, finally, and she knew he could not win this one alone. He needed them, his family, as he'd always needed them for his life, and we, she thought, we need you Sonny. Absurdly, sentimentally, and somehow completely appropriately, she heard herself singing lines from an old song, "He ain't heavy, he's my brother," and her heart caught somewhere between her chest and her throat.

She turned onto Hawley Avenue and saw the pale red brick of Iris Arms, a black and white sign in front of the building advertising rooms for rent, the scruffy little hill of grass and weeds looking dingy and brown, the cool cement steps, the iron railing leading up to the glass doors of the apartments. She had known exactly where it was, though she'd never been there: the women's bar was directly across the street.

Irony heaped itself upon irony this day, and she parked the car looking up at her brother's building through the haze of cold rain and the sky that seemed perpetually gray and foreboding. Rose had an urgent desire to call Deborah, wished Lorraine could have come with her. She felt desperately alone and realized that this was but a tiny hint of what Sonny must have experienced every day of his life since Momma's death. Again that twinge of guilt and shame. This time she yielded to it, letting it move through her body till it gave rise to a new clarity: the past had to take its place. Each of them had to begin looking at the start of some other way they could see each other. She had seen her father know just this in that moment of rage that moved toward recognition, had seen the ease with which Lorraine had entered the circle of her father's arms. It was her mother she thought of now, the lessons of seeing and forgiveness and love all making generosity of spirit what each of them had to learn, was learning. Rose prayed right then, really prayed, for the first time in years, full of conviction and sincerity. She prayed that Sonny would not have to be sacrificed for the lesson to take hold.

◆

What was she looking for? She had no idea, but when Sonny didn't answer her knock, she found the super and convinced him to open the door to Sonny's apartment. She had to admit to herself that though she hoped there would be something in there that would lead her to her brother, she was more than a little curious to see how he lived. She looked around his apartment noting its dinginess, the absence of anything she recognized of him. A drawer of the dresser was open, and Rose rummaged through it, through the unmatched socks and underwear, looking for anything, something personal.

She was struck deeply when she saw the edge of a photograph sticking out of the boxer shorts and socks; she pulled it out. It was the picture she'd taken of Sonny and her mother in front of a restaurant, Easter Sunday, how many years ago? Sonny was about thirteen. She saw her mother there in her

Easter suit, a corsage of carnations pinned to her left lapel,
her eyes distracted by something behind them, Sonny with his
arm loosely draped around his mother's shoulders, the two of
them, looking out at the camera as though they were tolerat-
ing its presence. And nothing else in the apartment could she
find that proved her brother lived there, just this single
photograph, thin around the edges as though it had been
fingered and held often, often.

She thanked the super and asked him, too, to call if he saw
Sonny.

Rose thought about the apartment and its lack of spirit.
The sensation she'd had looking at the picture of Sonny and
Josie told her the thing wrong with him went beyond the AV
malformation, was larger even than that, although probably
aggravated by it. It was as though she knew the instant she
found that picture, and nothing else of anyone, that Sonny's
world was that photograph, that he wanted Josie, and she
was dead. Rose thought now only of how Sonny was planning to be with her.

It was one forty-five. She sped to the hospital. If she could
see Moses O'Toole, maybe Sonny'd be there. Maybe this
Moses could help find him, and if not she could get to the
QuikStar around three, maybe get Sonny as he went to work.

thirty

HE GOT OUT OF THE CAB at the juncture of Routes 11 and 81 around four in the afternoon. The sky had darkened considerably, a kind of purplish gray, like a fading bruise, and a fine misty rain was falling. He was several long blocks from home, and he began walking slowly, a solitary figure, hands stuffed into the pockets of his overcoat, chin down on his chest, shoulders hunched up around his ears as though from the cold. His heart was breaking. He could feel bits and pieces of the ache cracking in splinters, like the small sounds of someone snapping wooden matchsticks again and again and again, and he attached to that feeling now the same disregard one would have for snapping matchsticks. It was simply happening.

Sometime in the last twenty-four hours Sonny and his body had reached a disjuncture. He was driven, it seemed, by a purpose apart from himself, yet it was only himself he was aware of. So long had he been cut off from his own need that once it was touched, it emerged with a force both violent and confusing, filled with the distortions of years of blighted light, always the small and brilliant glimmer followed by the hiss of meanness. His memories were turning on themselves, on him, fed as they were by the poisons floating through his mind, released when he finally realized that he *needed:* he needed love and touching. It was such an elemental need he had been cheated of, except from his Momma, and he couldn't find her in him. She drifted somewhere just out of his touch, growing unfocused in a thickening haze behind his eyes.

Oblivious even to the searing pain nearly constant in his right temple, over his right eye, Sonny moved through the streets, barely noticing the neat suburban tract houses, ranch style, each alike except for minor flairs: sometimes red shutters instead of black, the several designs of mailboxes, the occasional newspaper box, the rarer piece of lawn sculpture. The rain fell slowly and persistently on everything, misting Sonny's glasses, but he no longer relied entirely on them to see. He was driven only by his need to find the source of love in his life, headed in her direction, nothing else on his mind, his right hand still in his coat pocket, a feeling fierce and certain throbbing, echoing, in his otherwise cloudy head.

thirty-one

EVERY PATH LED NOWHERE. Moses O'Toole was semicoma-
tose, dying of lung cancer; he lay in his bed motionless and
silent and unaware of Rose's presence. The head nurse of his
floor told Rose that Moses O'Toole would probably not live
through the night. Yes, a man fitting Sonny's description had
been up to see him yesterday. Rose stood for a minute beside
Moses' bed, wondering once more about the turnings of her
brother's life, the people in it. How very little she knew or
understood Sonny DeMarco, her only brother, her flesh and
blood; how little she had genuinely cared about knowing or
understanding him had never seemed more clear.

Moses drew ragged, uneven breaths through the pale green
oxygen cannules in his nostrils, then didn't breathe: Cheynes-
Stokes respirations, an indicator of impending death. She
had to fight an urge to push at him, make him wake up, talk
to her, tell her about her brother. Rose was about to leave
when the man's eyes flew open filled with a look of terror, as
though he were waking from a nightmare. He was conscious
and asked for water, assuming Rose was a floor nurse. She
gave him a sip of the water on his bedside table, and when he
didn't lapse immediately back into that deep sleep, she told
him who she was, why she was there.

"He never said nothing bout no Rose," he spoke slowly, so
softly that she had to bend her head way down, until her ear

was practically against his mouth, to hear him. "Just his Momma, just always talked about his Momma. Said when the old man died, he was gonna live with her."

A clammy sweat broke out on Rose's body. Her chest constricted, and then a feeling like a quiet explosion spread through her. She swore she could feel her pupils widen in fear. "His Momma?" Rose stopped, remembering Sonny's voice on the telephone on Sunday. She looked at Moses, his gaunt and yellowed face, his labored breathing. "Moses." Rose was speaking quietly now, the shock of what she was hearing hushed her, drained almost all of the little energy she had left. "Moses, our Momma, Sonny—his Momma is dead. She's been dead for two years."

"Don't know nothin bout that." And he looked at her, his eyes hooking into hers, sure of what he was saying. She thought pity moved through his eyes. Then, unexpectedly, he reached up a bony, dry hand and brushed Rose's face. "Sonny favors you all right. He's a good boy, brought me this," he said pointing to the flask on the back of his bed stand, "but something's awful sad or mean in him. He called his Momma a lot. On Sundays. Said he was gonna be with her. Said forever could change. You find him, you send him here, you hear? I wanna tell him it can't, it can't change. Only one way it change." He took a breath, the sound harsh, raspy. Rose heard the slight hissing of the oxygen running, the steady drone of rain on the window of his room, the only light in the room coming in gray and gloomy through the window.

They were alone here. The second bed in Moses' room was empty, the white hospital bedspread drawn up as though to an invisible chin, the bed railing up on one side, down on the other, clearly waiting for its occupant. The sight of that waiting bed filled her with a terrible sense of foreboding. Moses said, so quietly and so very certainly, "You tell him it can't, cept one way. This way here. And you tell him he too young to die." And he was out as suddenly as he'd awakened, his eyelids fluttering for the briefest part of a second. Then he lay silent, his hand on Rose's went slack, and she took the dry and wrinkled hand and placed it on Moses' chest, standing just another minute before she turned and left.

◆

At three forty-five she emerged from the QuikStar, her stomach burning from the three cups of coffee she'd had waiting for Sonny to come to work. She was going to ask the counterman about her brother, had sat at the counter drinking the first cup, going over the scene with Moses in her head. She was taking in the fact that this was where Sonny worked, and she sat there with a deep sense of despair. Something told her he was not going to show up here today. She could hardly see him in here at all: the floors were grimy, a coat of grease permeated everything, the fluorescent lights buzzed relentlessly. And the guy behind the counter was sleazy. He eyed her through his beady sharp eyes when she came in, ran a hand over his slicked-down light brown hair, saying, "Can I help you?" in an oily voice. When he smiled at her, the smile revealed yellowed teeth. He wore a grimy tee shirt, blue jeans, a white apron; pinned to it was a blue pin with "Ron" on it. She almost hoped that Sonny wouldn't come in because she didn't want to see him near this creepy counterman. Rose couldn't bring herself to confide in him or ask him anything about her brother.

A Black woman and a white woman, both young, both dressed in high K Mart fashion, both heavily made up, sat at the opposite end of the counter, and this guy, this "Ron," fawned over them, flirted with them. He didn't notice how they rolled their eyes at each other when he turned around. Rose couldn't help grinning into her coffee cup at that. A

white man, probably in his forties, sat in a booth, drunk, a
half cup of coffee before him, his pants torn at both knees,
wearing a filthy, once-tan raincoat. Any other time Rose
would have felt conspicuously out of place and a little at risk,
but today that seemed irrelevant.

By three-twenty Sonny had not arrived, and Ron began
cursing him up and down, trying without success to evoke
some sympathy from the women at the counter. He started
making phone calls, looking for someone to work for him.
Rose gathered from listening to him on the phone that Sonny
and Moses both worked here. She figured Lucinda came in as
well. She waited and watched and said nothing to Ron.
Twenty-five minutes later, certain Sonny wasn't going to
show up, Rose laid a dollar on the counter and left. She
stopped a couple of blocks up at a phone booth and called
Deborah, told her what was happening and asked her to
come out to North Syracuse after work. Then she called
home. No one there had heard anything. She got back into
her car. There was nothing else she could think of to do but
go home and wait.

thirty-two

HE WAS IN THE BACKYARD, crouching behind two huge box elders about fifty feet from the kitchen window. Every now and then he could hear his father's voice raise up. Sonny had arrived around five, shortly after Rose had returned, soon after Deborah and Curtis got there. He knew nothing of any of this, had not noticed Rose's car parked across the street, did not know Curtis' or Deborah's cars to recognize them. Each time he heard his father's voice, anger coursed through him; he was certain Dominic was yelling at his mother, and had to fight an impulse to race through the back door.

But, no, he told himself, no, he was going to wait. He wanted to see her first; he was sure that sooner or later she would appear at the window over the sink in the kitchen. Through it, a golden cone of light shone out to the back yard. Sonny was patient. He waited silently, not minding the waiting at all, hardly noticing the wet, cold rain falling on him, flexing and unflexing his fingers around the knife in his pocket, occasionally grimacing, drawing his lips together hard, clenching his teeth when the sudden jolts of burning pain seared through his head. He was otherwise more at ease than he'd been in awhile, sure of this, only of this, the driving unmistakable need to get close to his mother.

Inside, they sat around the table, an odd assortment of people that made their own sense. While Rose had run around Syracuse, Lorraine had made a pot of sauce and meatballs; the smell filled the house. They were eating together, strangers and family, in the intimacy and comfort only crises can bring.

The biggest change was, of course, in Dominic. When he shook Curtis' hand and looked at his son-in-law, when he saw Donna with him, grown up already, he could only think of what he had missed, what he had deprived himself of. Try as he might, he could no longer come up with one good reason for having done that. And Deborah with Rose. Even that. He could see they loved each other, could see the way Deborah's eyes met Rose's as Rose returned home, tired, and how Deborah had brought her coffee without asking her if she wanted it. In that gesture he was reminded of Josie, and again his loss gripped him, his eyes filling with tears. But with the sensation of loss came something else. He began to understand his own responsibility, saw that he had to give love as well as expect to receive it, and though he used to think he had given love, he knew now it was a stunted version of what he was capable of.

They sat and ate and were quiet, or they argued: Rose and Lorraine thought Dominic should call Eddie Marino; Dominic was hesitant, but it was now out of a sense of protectiveness toward Sonny, even though he knew this was not the best time to be protective in that way. *He* wanted to find Sonny, though in his heart he was a little afraid. Having felt the intensity of his own emotions, he was beginning to get a glimmer of the force of Sonny's, and he realized that his son might not want to see him.

They all tensed when the phone rang, but it was Joe Rizzo checking to see if they'd located Sonny, telling them to call the minute they did. They sat for a while longer around the table, trying to come up with some plan, deciding at last to call Eddie. Rose first make her father promise to leave Lucinda out of it; she believed Lucinda and Adora had told her as much as they knew. Next she called Upstate, to the floor Moses was on, to see if Sonny had been there, then the QuikStar and Lucinda. Rose came away from the phone with nothing new.

And still they sat there, closer than they'd ever been, their need and love for one another out in the open; yet never had any of them felt so helpless. They wanted to believe that the intensity of their feelings was enough to in some way draw Sonny back home, into the circle. They could not know that it had, that right at this moment Sonny was so near, crouched and waiting for a sign; that he had undergone his own profound change, an altering of vision; that he thought of none of them in the old way. They were almost completely inconsequential.

As he hid in the back yard a swirl of memories floated over his head like a flock of hovering birds. He could not know and probably would not believe that his mother's spirit had finally begun to surface in the rest of his family, for nothing in his lifetime had shown him that possibility. That same spirit in himself, his driving force for so long, was now dangerously submerged. What had been his nature had become a symbol: the idea of rather than the feeling for his mother was now what moved him.

Did Sonny do anything out there in the encroaching darkness, the constant fine cold rain like a curtain sheer and opalescent at once, diamonds of pale reds and yellows and a milky blue moved from his eye to the house, to that oval of light, pale golden, a beacon familiar and comforting as a lighthouse in storm, deep in the night's belly? He did nothing but wait and watch with the fiercest energy, understanding through the window that was home and his own mind that once more he was outside and alone, but that that period was coming to a close.

Inside they were clearing the table, Curtis and Lorraine trying to decide whether to spend the night here or return home.
Either way, Curtis thought it would be a good idea for him to
cruise around downtown to look once more for Sonny; Lorraine or Rose would have to go with him, since Curtis had
never seen his brother-in-law. While they talked, Dominic sat
at the head of the old mahogany table, smoking, watching
them, his eyes moving over Junior, who slept on the living
room floor as though he'd always been there. Rose filled the
sink with hot water and began to do the dishes. In the back
yard Sonny watched from his lookout spot between the trees
and saw motion around the window. He crept closer, bent
low, moving silently, his shoes, his pants, all of him really
quite soggy by now, all the time watching that window. He
saw the steam from the sink billow up, cloud the glass.

Rose was exhausted, yet all the tension was gone from her.
She moved slowly, wanting a hot bath, to get rid of the
uniform she still wore; it felt sticky, clinging to her after a day
that seemed endless. She enjoyed doing the dishes, the hot
water a comfort on her skin. She let it run, drifting with this
chore, dreamlike, noticing nothing beyond it for the moment, feeling it almost like a luxury, a breathing space in a
time filled otherwise with urgency and need. The shussing
sound of the water, the quiet and persistent hiss of the slow
rain, the feel of the warm, sudsy water and the steam of it was
like a dream along her forearms.

He was watching, watching, mesmerized by what he saw
and felt through the window, his mind a jumble of feeling
and sensation and thoughts flitting and jumping but always
returning to his own need, raw and vulnerable and passionate, waiting for the moment to reveal himself.

*"She is in here, she has to tell you something," Aunt Louise
in a dream, was it a dream, saying, "Here, Sonny, she is in
here, she has to tell you something." And he saw only a wom-*

an he knew so well and couldn't place, a woman strong, a woman standing at a sink in a white blouse doing dishes. He heard the shussing sound of the water running, could see the steam rising up over the sink, in front of this woman whose face he couldn't see yet, who radiated with the necessity of the message, and panic rose in him fierce as thunder. He watched her arms go in and out of the water, saw her shoulders slender and weary, her hair pulled back, the blackness of it streaked heavily with an iron gray, and she was about to turn and beckon him.

She dried her hands, reached up her arms in a stretch, ran her hands through her dark hair, streaked with gray, so like her mother in appearance and gesture just then that Dominic looking over at her felt flooded with emotion. He got up and walked toward the kitchen, not sure yet of what he was doing. He only knew he wanted to be nearer, so he picked up some stray silverware and his coffee cup to carry to the sink

Aunt Louise saying, "Maybe not yet, Sonny, you don't have to go to her, you can wait, you can wait awhile," but no he couldn't wait, had been waiting too long *and he turned out there in the yard, soaking wet and beginning to shiver, colors and shapes dancing before his eyes, merging always with the gold light from the window, and of course it was his Momma, but not in the dream, here, right here, just beyond the window in that beacon of light he could now remember always following, sparkling and golden as the chalice at mass, and he rose full up out of the crouch*

She thought she saw something move out there in the yard and leaned closer to the window, squinting to see,

away from secrecy and mystery and denial, and staring into that window at the woman, his Momma, standing at the sink doing dishes, her arms upraised to greet, to welcome him, the sign he waited for, and it was time. Aunt Louise was wrong. He did have to go, it was time, her face leaning to him and just then Dominic was there, saying "Here, Rosie," handing her more dishes, and she turned to him

and it was too much for him. He could not watch another betrayal, yet before his eyes he saw her turn from him, from the sink to his father when it was he who needed her now. He was past thinking, just felt himself moving steadily toward the house, toward the window, then off to his right toward the back door, and he opened it. His eyes were burning, and he trembled and stumbled and clutched the fishing knife in his pocket, drawing it out, opening it, the blade flashing in the night

They all heard the door open and froze for a second, heard the shuffling, almost dragging footsteps, and still were not prepared to see Sonny. He was what they'd all been waiting for, and yet when he burst in, wild-eyed, flashing a silver knife, each was speechless, each frozen in a posture of fear and terror and horror. He was soaking wet, dripping on the floor of the kitchen, giving off an odor of wet wool, and something else almost electric in its smell. In the next second his head was jerking from side to side, from person to person, looking desperately about him, brandishing that knife

and he couldn't see her, but he had seen her at that window. His eyes lit on his sister Rose's but couldn't stay there. What was this Lorraine and this baby sleeping on the floor and this Black man, and who was this girl. There were strangers here, and he looked at his father who was saying nothing, even in that like a stranger, and something began to click in his mind. He saw the empty cage of Tweety Three, and over there by the telephone he saw the bulletin board and the card of St. Lucy, and he knew nothing was as he thought it and couldn't bear that and even knowing that nothing was as he thought it, he raised up his right hand, the glint of silver arcing through the air, and was heading toward Dominic. From the corner of his eye he saw the Black man moving

*toward him and more, he saw his father did not move, did
not draw up his fists, and he was more confused than he'd
ever been. Now Rose, Lorraine, this Black man, they were
moving toward him, it seemed in slow motion as he watched
it. But he knew it was faster than that, oh so much faster, and
he waved the knife dangerously fast and let out a howl like
nothing he had ever heard or felt before, wanting to keep
them away and wait. His father was moving toward him, his
hand now out in some strange gesture, and Sonny lunged at
him, but then it was Rose moving, and where was she who
had stood at the sink, who had beckoned to him in the motion he had seen, her arms up calling him. The Black man was
moving, and in a flash he saw a blur of Rose, hating her for
not being who he'd seen at the window. He screamed again, a
horrible sound he could hear apart from himself, and someone else was screaming in the distance. Dominic was too
close, kept reaching out his hand, and it was through the
knife he held, the only way, and he held it tight, feeling every
fiber in him tensed and growling, his teeth bared, his lips
drawn way back, his eyes blazing. He feinted with the knife,
held them at bay, backed away out of there and was running
into darkness.*

thirty-three

IT WAS AFTER MIDNIGHT, and he was leaning against the wall of Mr. Link's garage. He could hear the rain still falling. The wind had picked up; it howled through the cracks around the doors. He was cold, huddled on the cement floor, his coat pulled tightly around him, his head dropping against his chest every now and then, when he'd jerk it up with a shot of alarm, gripping once again the silver knife in his pocket. He sat there thinking to himself: they should have known. He had heard Curtis and Rose calling him as he sped away from the house, heard Curtis yell, "the car," knew they were chasing after him right now, and a bitter little grin twitched at the corners of his mouth: they should have known.

When he was a kid he had run away once. He couldn't remember why; maybe he wouldn't eat his dinner, or he had sassed his father, or something had scared him, and he had been off in a dash, hiding out for hours in old Mr. Link's garage, just a couple of blocks from home, a garage that had once been a barn, standing back a ways from the street, separate from Mr. Link's house, with a side door, like the door to a house, that was never locked. They had found him finally, after searching the neighborhood, had found him asleep on the floor, a pile of old newspapers for a pillow. They should have known. He had raced here tonight on instinct, not thinking of anything except the need for safety, running away from home again to the one spot he could recall, as though no time had passed between, as though nothing had changed in the years between hideouts.

Iris Arms had been a hideout. He knew he wouldn't be going back there after tonight. Rose would talk with Lucinda to try and find him, he was sure of that, and Lucinda was the one person who knew where he lived. He thought she'd try to cover for him, but still, it was no longer his own. The thought of Lucinda and Dawn made him feel almost homesick for a second, and he touched his chest. What was it? He sat in the dark squinting, trying to remember something. What was it? It seemed as though snatches of conversations were floating over his head, flitting through his mind. The homesickness made his chest ache, a strange curve of desire. He remembered little of the details of what had just happened, of what he'd run from, and saw memories of it like snapshots: the empty cage of Tweety Three, his father's strange gesture toward touching him, the gray steam billowing up over his Momma as she washed dishes. He thought of seeing people in the house he did not recognize, and that thought made his skin almost creep in humiliation. His eyes in his mind kept turning to his left, to that card on the bulletin board, St. Lucy. He could see the arms out, holding the dish, that dish with her eyes. Like a dream he remembered it and thought again, what was it he was stretching to get back to. What was it Lucinda had said to him the last time he saw her—something about church on Saturday—but that didn't make sense. He leaned against the gray cold cement wall feeling the dampness of it through his sweatshirt and wool jacket. "Don't forget," she had said, "she told you not to forget St. Vincent's on the twenty-first. At nine o'clock. Said you'd know what she meant." Well dammit, he didn't remember. Sonny tensed, his heart beginning to race, not thinking clearly about anything but the fact that once again he was alone, all of them missing the signal. A slow and murky rage built in his chest, his belly, and nothing would come clear except the rage and a sense of loss, and a flame of red dancing, jumping every now and then before his eyes.

At the first light of dawn Sonny woke with a start, unsure at first of where he was, or why he was there. He shook his head, trying to clear it, to remember what had gone on. It came back to him slowly, and in reverse: the sound of his running footsteps on wet pavement; the voices calling after him in the night; then, like a dream unraveling, he recalled standing in the dining room of his house, his father's strange silence, the odd gesture of his hand reaching out to him, and not in a way meant to strike. Rose, Lorraine, his mother standing at the sink doing dishes, and the holy card with a date: November 21. He pushed the hair away from his eyes; it was damp with cold sweat. He grimaced at something, then slid his hand into his pocket and was reassured for a moment. In his other pocket was his key ring, and on it, next to his own apartment key, was the one to Moses' apartment. Moses' place would be safe for at least a couple of days, he thought. He got up, the headache almost completely gone, quietly opened the door, and stood facing the back of the garage, pissing. A fine cold rain was still falling, the sky dense with clouds. Sonny was cold and hungry and wanted coffee. He touched his face, thick with a growth of beard, zipped up his pants, and stealthily made his way out of Mr. Link's yard, collar up, head tucked down to his chest. He walked to the junction of the highways where the cab had let him out yesterday, taking the first bus back into Syracuse.

Something had snapped whatever control he had had over events, and memories had flown like a kite cut from its line when he'd stood with the knife in the dining room, or sometime in the back yard as he'd crouched and waited for a sign. It was almost as though his life, this Sonny DeMarco's life, was just beginning. That blur of memory and emotion and raw need that was his past formed a diminishing vee, like migrating birds. His mother had turned from him, but he knew she was not to blame, not St. Patience, she who had prayed all those years to St. Lucy for vision. She was not to be held responsible, he could see now, could see it all. He remembered telling Moses that day, it seemed so long and dark ago, that forever could change, and it had. Sonny's forever had changed, and though he thought he saw that clearly now, he could no longer see into himself. He caught only faint and fleeting glimpses of the gold cone of light that had led him, and the memory of his mother stood off to a side of his vision, more like a statue of a saint on the dashboard of a car — flimsy, tilted, and slightly grimy and pale from sunlight and neglect — more like that than of an emotion that drove him.

On the bus ride back to Syracuse, Sonny felt a mean and intense energy moving through his body, and he thought he was in control. His body, his mind, and his brain were conspiring against him, were revolting against those years of resignation and misery, were taking over all that he had been. The sun began its arc up the sky, breaking the clouds after long days of fog and rain, and he took that as a sign in his favor.

thirty-four

"ROSE...ROSE...YA BETTER wake up." Curtis was nudging her shoulder gently, a cup of coffee in his other hand.

Rose's eyelids shot open. For a brief second she did not know where she was: she looked around at the pale green walls, saw the shattered light fixture, and remembered. She and Curtis were in Moses O'Toole's room at the Clinton Hotel, hoping that Sonny would show up. They'd checked all the other places he might have been, had talked again with Lucinda, and even with Ron Jenkins at the QuikStar. Eddie Marino had been called in, and Uncle Tony and Dominic were out with him looking for Sonny. Deborah and Lorraine were holding the fort at home with Uncle Sal, in case Sonny returned there.

Any reservation Curtis held onto about his wife's sister had disappeared in that moment when both of them sprang toward the door, responding to a similar instinct to go after Sonny. There occurred between them the kind of closeness that most often happens between strangers, when there is nothing to lose or risk. They'd talked well into the night, drinking coffee, sitting, at first quietly, each of them savoring the break in tension that Moses' room allowed them. After awhile, Rose said, "Curtis, I'm glad I met you. It's one of the good things that this has let happen. I mean, I'm glad it brought me and Lorraine back together, and Lorraine and Pop, and meeting you, and Junior...well...." Her voice trailed off.

Curtis smiled. "Me too, Rose. At first, you know, I thought Lorraine was crazy, letting you back just like that." He snapped his fingers. "But, you know Lorraine." He stopped, looking at Rose, "Don't you? I'll probably never understand why you stayed away from her, drugs or no drugs, but Lorraine's awfully glad you're back. And, I guess I am, too. We can start from here. None of us gets it right all the time."

They had talked till early morning, sitting on Moses' couch, until each of them dozed off. Now, Rose sat up, stretched, and began talking through a yawn. "Oh, God, Curtis, what time is it?" She took the coffee. "Thanks," she said, and repeated, "what time is it?"

"Close to seven. What do you think we oughta do?"

"I have no fucking idea." She was almost giddy from tension and lack of sleep. More than anything right now she wanted a bath, and to get out of the uniform she still wore. She drank her coffee, waking up, trying to clear her head.

Curtis walked over to the window. "It's stopped raining. Looks like the sun's gonna come out. That's a good sign." He took a pick from his pants pocket, absent-mindedly working it through his hair. He looked at her. "Don't ya think it's a good sign?"

"Hunh." She met his eyes. "A good sign of what?"

"I don't know. Just not so gloomy, I guess."

"That's something." She finished her coffee. "I think we should check in at my father's, see how everybody's doing there, and I want to go home and change—I feel like I've lived too long in this uniform—and I have to call the hospital. Do you have to call in at work?" Curtis nodded. "Right now, I have to go to the bathroom." She got up. Passing the table in the kitchenette, she glanced at the photograph hanging on the wall. "Who do you suppose that is?"

"I don't know, maybe it's his girlfriend. I don't know the guy." Curtis looked at the picture. "Got a nice smile, though."

"Yeah. She looks familiar to me." And she remembered Moses reaching up, touching her face, saying, "Sonny favors you all right."

Her eyes filled with tears in this dingy room with the sun coming in and the picture of a woman who favored Moses, a smile that just at this moment seemed full of a hope that Rose wanted to feel. Whoever the woman in the picture was, she was someone in Moses' life, a man she didn't know at all, yet for whom her heart ached. She wondered if the woman knew about him, if right now she was sitting next to his bedside, touching his dry and dying hand. She remembered that empty bed and knew she couldn't even imagine her own brother's life. Rose felt bereft, a deep and awful sense of loneliness and despair that the emerging sun made more acute. Suddenly she was sobbing like a little kid, the kind of sob that catches in your throat hours after the act of crying is over, crying for every sadness she'd ever known, every one she might have caused, crying for Sonny, who, too, might be dying. Curtis stood there for a second, taking her in, and reached out his hand. Then he stopped himself from the little gesture, and put his arms around her saying, "cry, Rosie," calling her by the family nickname. And she did cry, thankful for Curtis, wishing for her mother and the sight of her kid brother, and for something, something simple, for them all.

When they left, neither of them noticed the bulky figure who turned the corner and headed toward the Clinton, nor his sudden stop and awkward about-face. They got into their car and drove off in the opposite direction.

thirty-five

AFTER EVERYONE HAD LEFT, Uncle Sal came over to "stay with the girls," as Dominic put it; Lorraine, Deborah, and Donna sat around the kitchen table. Junior had finally fallen off to sleep, and Sal lay on the couch in the living room, snoring loudly.

Donna was still shaken by what she had witnessed. Once Sal fell asleep, she asked, "But what's *wrong* with Uncle Sonny?" Her face was pale, her light brown hair kept falling across her eyes, dark brown, and wide with confusion and fear.

"He's sick, honey." Lorraine stroked her daughter's head. "He has something wrong with his brain, Donna. It's making him act different."

"But he didn't even look at me. And he looked so awful."

"Yeah, he did. That's why everyone's out trying to find him. He probably didn't recognize you. He hasn't seen you in a long time. He never saw Junior. Or Curtis. I wonder what he thought."

"Did he ever see you?" Donna looked at Deborah, who'd been silently watching them talk, slowly sipping another cup of coffee.

"Yeah, a couple of times. But not for awhile now."

"Are you Rosie's girlfriend?" Donna asked this question, suddenly shifting the conversation.

Deborah was caught off guard. She glanced over at Lorraine, who smiled, and nodded her head just slightly.

"Yes," she answered.

"Do you live in the same house?"

"No."

"Why not?"

"Oh, I don't know." Deborah felt as though she was being interviewed. Donna had startled her. She acted as though she knew that she and Rose were lovers, and though Deborah was not one to talk about it much, it seemed like enough stuff about all of them was coming to light this night that Donna's questions were appropriate. She relaxed and looked at her lover's niece. "We kind of like it just the way it is."

"Oh."

They sat quietly for a few minutes, Uncle Sal's snoring and the light splatter of rainfall the only sounds. It was the middle of the night, and while Sal was able to sleep, the three of them were wide awake, though exhausted, and were drawn to one another, to the kitchen table and this slow conversation.

"You know," Lorraine said, "even though Sonny's been so big for awhile now, it always surprises me when I see him. He used to be such a scrawny thing, little pigeon chest, skinny little legs. He used to throw his supper behind the couch." She smiled to herself, more than to Deborah or Donna. "Doesn't look like he does that much anymore."

"Rose says the same thing. And I can't picture him skinny. You want more coffee?" Deborah stood up to get a refill.

"No thanks," Lorraine and Donna answered in unison. "Wait," Lorraine got up, "let me see if I can find some pictures."

She went into the bedroom, the room that used to be Dominic and Josie's, and was struck by the scent of her mother's perfume, the same bedspread, the wedding picture on the bureau. A wave of grief and loss hit her: she hadn't been in this room for years, and it felt as though her mother had never left it.

In a few minutes she came out with the photo albums she had been searching for, and the three of them pulled their chairs close together, the albums stacked in the center of the table. Lorraine sat in the middle of Deb and Donna, narrating. "Look," she said, "here's a picture of Sonny when Pop bought him that baseball suit. I think it was his fourth birthday." And there was a skinny little boy wearing a New York Yankees pinstripe baseball suit, his cap too large for him. It was slanted off to his right and gave him a confused appearance rather than a rakish one. He was holding a baseball bat, a small smile on his face, and his eyes looking out of the picture seemed to plead for something.

"*That's* Uncle Sonny?" Donna was incredulous.

"That's my brother Sonny." Lorraine *knew* that kid; Donna and Deborah had to take it on faith. It seemed funny to Lorraine, funny and poignant. She touched the face in the picture, remembering the softness of Sonny's skin, the silky texture of his thick black hair. She flipped forward several pages. "Here he is again. Recognize him now?"

"Jesus, what a scene. Who's the girl?" Deb stared at the picture: "Sonny and Linda, Senior Prom, 1973," was printed beneath it. Sonny stood in a double-breasted black tuxedo, a hefty boy wearing black glasses, his hair brushed neatly, his arm awkwardly draped over the shoulder of Linda, a chubby, blonde girl in a yellow taffeta gown, a green ribbon making an empire waistline. She wore a wristlet of yellow roses and was smiling widely. In Sonny's lapel was a yellow carnation.

"That's Linda, Sonny's girlfriend. Well, she used to be his girlfriend; they went to high school together. I don't know what happened to her. Pop used to call her a cow. I wonder what went on with them. I think Sonny really liked her."

"How come you don't know, Mom?" Donna kept trying to make some sense out of everything she was learning tonight.

"Because, kiddo, I didn't talk to anybody for awhile. I told you: I was a snot and your grandfather was a bigger snot. I don't know, maybe we were too much alike, always looking for a good time." She paused. She'd never really talked to Donna about what it was like growing up, and even if she wanted to, she found it almost impossible to explain it in words. So much of what had gone on as they all lived together was feeling, emotion that had its own language, that lost its texture in speech. She knew that every time she tried to talk with Curtis about it, the stories sounded like so much detail, and nothing more.

The best way she knew how to "talk" about it was explained by the way she felt when she'd walked back into the house yesterday. Looking at Rose and Dominic, years of feeling had welled up in each of them, and it was only through the feelings that they were able to remember and forgive at once. Or like the way she felt going into her parents' bedroom tonight—the room seemed to emanate memory and emotion, an almost overpowering sensation—palpable and rich, and, as with most memories Lorraine had of the family, over them all hovered a filmy cloud of longing that made her chest ache. She looked at her daughter. Donna was tired and confused, and suddenly very young. Lorraine put her arm around her shoulders and Donna let herself be held like a little girl again, leaning into her mother. She yawned, finally relaxed for a moment, and was all at once overcome with tiredness. "Why don't you go lie down, Donna. We'll wake you up if we hear anything. Okay?" She looked at the clock. It was three in the morning.

"Promise?" Donna asked.

"Promise." Lorraine crossed her heart.

172 Rachel Guido deVries

"All right then." Donna kissed Lorraine on the cheek and headed off to one of the bedrooms, then stopped, turned around, looked at Deborah, and shyly came back and kissed her, too, on the cheek. "G'night, Deborah. You gonna wait for Rosie?"

"Yes. I'll see you in the morning Donna. Sleep good."

Alone, Lorraine looked at Deborah. "Tired?"

"Exhausted. But I don't think I could fall asleep."

"Me neither. I wonder how Curtis and Rose are doing." Lorraine shook her head slowly, thinking. Then she looked up, changing the mood. "How did you meet Rosie?"

"I went to a photography show she had at the women's center a couple of years ago. A friend of mine introduced us."

"Are you a photographer, too?"

Deb chuckled. "No. I have an antiques place downtown. Do you have a job, I mean besides taking care of your family?"

"No. I used to do factory work. But since I married Curtis I haven't worked. It's kind of nice," she grinned, "I needed a rest after all the junk I did. And we really don't need the money. She shook her head again, looking at Deborah. "This is quite a family, isn't it?"

"I guess they all are—families. They're all different from what we're supposed to believe, you know, the picture of perfection, everybody getting along, like "The Donna Reed Show," or "Leave It To Beaver." But someplace in each of them there's usually a little love. You're lucky, in a way: this one's got more than usual."

"I guess," said Lorraine, "but it took us long enough to see it. I just hope Sonny has the chance to feel it."

It had stopped raining. The two women sat in the kitchen talking quietly, or were silent. Neither wanted to mention what would happen if he didn't.

thirty-six

HE WAS SO TIRED. He lay stretched out on the bed in a cheap motel room on the outskirts of the city, fully dressed, arms under his head, his glasses on. He was thinking. His thoughts were remarkably calm, and he was very confused.

When he saw his sister Rose come out of the Clinton Hotel with a Black man, he acted without thinking, getting himself to a taxi stand and this motel in a kind of blur of survival, and right now, just as whenever Sonny felt threatened, his survival depended desperately on solitude. In this solitude, in the quiet of the room, which was painted a pale pink, he lay atop the olive green corduroy bedspread, the curtains drawn. Still the melancholy sunlight that follows storms and gray skies urged itself through the small opening of curtain. He got up once, walking unsteadily over to the curtains and tried to pull them closer, to darken the room. Finally, he took a ball point pen and used its pocket clip to hold the curtain edges together. This helped a little. He lay back down and ate the cream donuts he'd bought at the Donut Delite across the street, dipping each bite into his coffee first.

He wasn't sure what he was doing, why he was here. He had no idea why Rose and Curtis had been at the Clinton and knew he couldn't go back to the QuikStar, but he was unsure why. He felt as though there was a kind of screen between this person that he was right here in this very second in time, which seemed so strangely to be the only one he had ever really known, and the rest of his life. He *knew* about the rest of his life; he simply could not feel it, could not make it come real. Even the thought of Moses in the hospital left him oddly cool at his center.

And whatever he'd been doing out there at his father's house was a puzzle to him. The parts he remembered stood out in bold relief, almost as though they were being played on the wall of his room as he lay there thinking: his mother, as always in his mind, in all of his thoughts, even now; the angle of light that made the only sense he knew, that image, that golden light within him was receding to a pinpoint of color, blurred and growing more obscure by the clutter of detail, fear and pain and sorrow rearranging itself in his head. The red blur of pain kept shooting out, stretching across his forehead, blazing behind his right eye. He was here. He was, for awhile at least, safe, and yet he felt the fear move in him like the sensation of illness in his belly, felt his feet, his arms go cold with it. He was so confused, so tired, so trapped, and he couldn't seem to get an idea to emerge.

◆

He was locked into a strange house. It was after midnight, and he was crouched on the floor of an upstairs bedroom, just beneath the window. He could see the navy blue sky, the stars, the moon—full and seeming to scowl at him. The stars, too, blinked hostility. He had to get out, but this was impossible unless he could figure out a way to unlock the front door from the outside. He knew he couldn't show his face at the window or the door so he was trying to think fast, to figure out a way out without showing himself. It was clear also in the dream that if he could do that, he would be out of danger, that the moon and the stars would stop hating him, that the ominous blue sky would soften, that he could be free.

He found a rope and a hook, fastened them together, and began dropping the rope to the front door right below the window of the room he was in, fishing, desperately trying to hook the doorknob and open the door from the outside. He was crouching, dangling the hook blindly, for to show his face, to lean out the window was certain death, he knew this, and he couldn't get it. The hook would brush the doorknob and slip away. He couldn't get out, and he was running out of time.

He crouched there terrified and nearly hopeless with his heart pounding in his chest, the moon beginning to show its rage, turning red, a huge round and angry ball of snarling toward him, and he couldn't get it. He couldn't get it. He wanted to get out of the house he was in that he had never seen before though he knew its secrets, all save the most important, and he couldn't get out without showing his face. He knew he was almost out of time. In the dream he could hear the ticking of seconds passing, and it grew louder, thunderous, the pressing and pounding of the time he was losing, the circle of moon taunting him, still the hook would not catch.

He felt the nausea well up from so deep within him. He was sweating, a cold horrible sweat of terror, of panic, and he wanted to stand up, make a run for it, but he couldn't. He wanted to ask, even to beg for more time, for another way, but he couldn't. It was too late. The motion of time stopped. Suddenly he heard its awesome silence, and the moon rolled in toward him from the sky, red and on fire, and he was in such danger his mind stopped working. He opened to the rage hurtling toward him. He opened his mouth to holler and instead breathed in the most furious air he had ever known, could never have imagined, and it seared him on the inside. It was consuming him, making him part of something he didn't want, but he had stopped fighting with it. And still the nausea as almost a thing apart from himself, writhing with it, the rage and burning pain and the need to throw up taking over, and what was his head was on fire with a throbbing violent spasm, shooting sparks like those hostile stars through his body and he gagged

He leapt from the bed, sobbing and gagging and vomiting before he reached the bathroom, not knowing what had just happened, what the danger was he'd been dreaming of, full of a terror that was wide awake now, that squinted against the smallest glimmer of light coming in the room. He was out of hope unless he could escape, and he had no idea from what.

◆

Sonny didn't wake up until Friday morning. He felt better. The nausea was gone, and all the hours of sleep had restored his spirits. He barely noticed the constant dull throbbing of his head. It had begun to rain again; the gray sky and rain calmed him further. It was eleven o'clock. He got up, went to the bathroom, saw the three days growth of beard on his face, and grinned at the sinister, seedy image of himself appearing in the mirror.

He threw on his coat and left the room, stopping at the motel office to keep the room for another couple of nights. He was glad that he'd taken all of his money with him; he had about eight hundred dollars in his pants pocket.

At a coffee shop near the motel he ate an omelet, home fries, and coffee, and read the paper, hardly thinking at all. He enjoyed the first calm moments he'd had in awhile, for once not thinking or planning, not moving backward into memory or forward into imagination or hope or retribution. He just sat there complacent, drinking his coffee.

When he left, he walked aimlessly, slowly, not minding the slow cold rain at all, oblivious to the splatters on his glasses. He saw a clothing store, went in, barely conscious of what he was doing or why he was doing it. He bought a white shirt, a pair of black polyester pants, a gray and black speckled tie, three pairs of boxer shorts, black socks. Next, he stopped at the drugstore and got a razor and blades, shaving creme, Old Spice aftershave, a tube of Brylcreme, copies of *Playboy* and *Hustler* and *Oui*. His final stop was at the P&C, where he picked up a loaf of Italian bread, a pound each of salami and provolone cheese, a six-pack of Coke, making a mental note to get ice when he returned to his room. Sonny was nesting and making plans for Saturday at the same time.

Back in his room, he hung his new clothes on hangers, arranged his groceries on the dresser, flipped on the TV, laid the magazines on the bed, stripped off his clothes, and took a long shower. When he came out he shaved, put on a new pair of boxer shorts, and lay on the bed, reading, watching TV, eating, or drinking his soda, feeling safe, drifting dreamily through his magazines, everything else on hold, shunted off to a side of his picture. His dream was forgotten. Why he was there he did not think about at all.

thirty-seven

EARLY MORNING FLOATED IN on him like a dream he was unsure of, and rocking in his strange bed, he knew desire was
warming for the long run. He'd slept for hours, the drum-
ming of his heartbeat an echo of a former time that moved
and merged with this time now, the perfect rhythm finally
moving through his blood stream till he rose, saying *of
course,* feeling his blood throb toward the definition of something he wanted to call pleasure, but knew in his blue, blue
heart that pleasure was a word that had changed meaning
sometime in some distant sleep. Now the clouds were parting
to that other time, that sometime, beginning to reveal a
mystery that was no longer a secret. The clouds parted and
the mystery unveiled the darkness when the stars blinked
many colors and moved into morning, a gray thing full of
rain and dull throbbing that echoed passion.

Twice, voices had called up the empty streets of his dreaming, and both in a language unclear; it was as though he needed a codeword. Yet even without it he was beginning to move
into another realm.

Certain finally of nothing but the motions he was making,
he could rise and stretch and yawn and shower and shave and
drink coffee. Then he dressed with a care, with a caution he'd
long been away from, feeling the texture of each item of
clothing he put on. Everything was new, and he sniffed each

piece before donning it, engaged now in the senses, alone, and full of the solemnity and pleasure of the occasion.

He pulled on each new sock slowly. He changed his shorts. He unfolded the black pants from the hanger and drew them on. He put on the white crisp cotton shirt, knotted his tie carefully into a double windsor, slipped on his loafers, and went back into the bathroom to brush his hair again. He checked for stray whiskers but was clean shaven. Sonny was gleaming and smelling of Dial soap and Old Spice and Brylcreme, and something else, some nearly animal scent that rose from him — the scent of excitement that is almost sexual, almost cedarlike and not at all unpleasant, but edged with tension and direction. He took his pills. He counted his money, rolling the bills into a careful fold as he'd seen his father do: the smallest bills on top, the profiles on the bills each facing the same direction, and he placed the fold into his right rear pocket. He scooped the change from the dresser top and put it into his right side pocket. He put his pocket comb into his left rear pocket. He was almost ready. "St. Vincent's on the twenty-first at 9:00 a.m.," Lucinda had said. He looked at himself again in the mirror.

He put on his coat, checking the right pocket for that safe silver flash against his fingers and moved out into the gray and rainy morning, a dreamy look behind his glasses, peering about him for a place to get a cab. "St. Vincent's at nine on the twenty-first," Lucinda had said, "they hope you'll be there." He smiled and was on his way.

◆

Rose, Lorraine, Donna, and Deborah were all crowded around the dresser mirror in the bedroom that used to be Sonny's, combing their hair, adjusting their clothes, quiet and solemn, and each very tired. The North Syracuse house had become a base for them all, each sleeping in shifts in Sonny's room or the parlor, on the couch or the floor. Curtis was in the bathroom; Uncle Sal and Uncle Tony fidgeted in the kitchen.

In the other bedroom, Dominic and Josephine's, Dominic was alone. By unspoken agreement, only he'd used that room, and he sat there now, on the edge of the blue satin bedspread, full of emotion—an uncertain dread and a vague confusion. The early gray skies depressed him further, and he looked over at the dresser at the wedding picture of himself with his bride, his Josephine, whom he was now on his way to publicly mourn and pray for for the second time since her death. His heart ached and felt so tender, and in his eyes was the flat and dejected and very solemn sadness of a man resigned to himself after too many years of fighting and avoiding and fending off that which might hurt. The morning had entered him with a damp and cold chill of foreboding that he was unable to shake off, that filtered into his all-at-once vulnerable heart as though his chest were a sieve, letting in the constant and slow motion of the rain, a natural rhythm that was his mood, that he didn't try to ignore, that hurt him so deeply he thought his heart would break.

Slowly, certainly, each member of this spent household migrated to the kitchen. They spoke very little, very quietly, their mourning and their sadness made more palpable by their inability to locate Sonny. A little thrill of fear glinted in everyone's chest and flitted in their eyes and hovered in the air around them. Each hoped Sonny would be there; each was also terrified by their last glimpse of him. More than anything else, each of the DeMarcos wished with all their hearts that Josephine was with them in life.

At eight-fifteen on Saturday morning, November 21, Rose spoke. "We'd better get going. I'll drive your car, Poppa. We can all fit except Uncle Tony and Uncle Sal." She looked over at her uncles. "And you two drive together, okay?" They nodded, relieved that Rose had taken charge.

They all left, the uncles driving off first in their car. The rest of them got into Dominic's dark blue Cadillac with the Blessed Mother serene on the dashboard, quiet, the rain falling persistently, the car's doors closing with a kind of finality to the outside air.

◆

Father Michael Valente was getting ready for the daily mass, the mass that today was to be offered in the name of and for the soul of Josephine DeMarco. He was the pastor of St. Vincent's now, and had been at the church for almost twenty-five years: first as a young curate, then assistant pastor, and now, as pastor. Although this mass was normally said by his assistant, Father Michael had agreed to offer it for the DeMarco family.

Of all of them, only Josephine had been a regular mass-goer. He remembered, though, how Rose had had a brief flurry of devotion to the church right around her confirmation, how she used to come with her mother and with her kid brother, Sonny. Rose stopped in to see him every now and then, and though he knew Dominic very casually, and most familiarly through his annual donation to the church, there was something about the DeMarcos he continued to feel warmly toward.

At eight-thirty he walked to the vestibule of the church, waiting for the family to arrive. He saw them drive up and get slowly from their car. He watched Rose and Dominic looking around the church for someone. Sonny was not with them.

◆

"What time is it?" Sonny had had a hard time getting a cab; he was a little nervous, anxious to be on time. Now he leaned over the back seat, looking at the cabbie.

"Five to nine," the cabbie replied. "You late?"

"I'm going to be. I've got to be at St. Vincent's at nine."

"Somebody getting married?" The cabbie, a young blond man, met Sonny's eyes in the rear view mirror.

Something skittered in his chest, and a lump rose up in his throat and took him by surprise. He swallowed hard against it; his eyes were burning. *Married,* he thought, and for a second he had absolutely no idea of what the word meant, but a swirl of emotion moved through his body. He thought he smelled incense and had a taste in his mouth of those little candy-coated almonds, although he knew those were not the sensations he'd experienced this morning getting ready for church. As he sat in the back of the cab there was something he sensed in the distance, a kind of fog he put around himself. The cabbie's question loosed something in him. It moved through the air and touched his skin, made him aware of feeling, and he couldn't right now, couldn't allow the feeling.

The cabbie was repeating his question. "Somebody getting married?" He thought to himself, this one's a little weird. He'd seen Sonny's eyes go from being fixed on his own to a kind of glazed stare in the mirror.

Sonny started, saw the eyebrows of the cab driver drawn together, and he suddenly and surprisingly grinned. "Not really," he said quickly, and rolled his eyes. "But I have to be on time."

Two cars were ahead of them, and they were approaching a traffic light. Sonny saw the first car slow as the green shifted to amber, and in that golden split second he saw hands raising something else that was golden and the deepest grief spread its wings in the bowl of his chest. Sonny began to know where he was going, and with that knowledge the horror yielded to something else: the most startling sensation of peace settled in him, and the fog began its slow dissolving.

thirty-eight

BY THE TIME THE CAB pulled up in front of the church, it was nine-twenty, and Sonny had begun to sweat. Holding on to an outward sign of calm while he paid the cabbie, he got out awkwardly from the back seat of the cab, the cold and damp November air striking his face and clearing his head. He saw the blue Cadillac. Sonny felt almost light-headed; the ground beneath his feet seemed spongy, uncertain, and his steps, as he made his way toward the large doors of the church, were oddly springy. His head was tucked down, his right hand again homing to his coat pocket, the throbbing behind his eyes constant, unaltered. His heart began to pound.

An unnatural kind of quiet was in the air around him, the street deserted except for a steady light passing of traffic, the whirring of the tires increasing his feeling of fear. He pulled open the door almost in spite of himself, in spite of the glint of danger sparking on the inside of his chest and the uneven flapping that was his heart.

He pulled open the door and was awash in the scent of incense and ritual, his eyes sweeping over the gleaming pews before looking up, up towards the altar where Father Michael was preparing for the consecration. He took in nothing specific, was startled by flashes of color, of blacks and grays and blues. Sonny was unaware of faces turning toward him, of the light that leapt into Dominic's eyes, then faded and became a sharpening kind of terror; of Rose ready to leap to her feet but for Dominic's hand holding her, whispering, "wait a minute," hoping that Sonny would see him, see them all, and sit with them; of Lorraine, trying to make his eyes meet hers. He was so confused, a jumble of feeling and memory and sensation keeping him rooted to the spot near the door at the back of the church.

He took a short little step, stopped, looked up toward the altar where Father Michael was raising the chalice, and the golden light shining off it connected with his vision. He swayed for a split second when his mind cleared absolutely *and the light golden as the chalice at mass that last time in November,* and he remembered everything. He saw his mother's coffin in front of the altar like that other time, knew he had done this before, that other time, knew with his last bit of thinking that his mother was dead. Something fluttered and moved and escaped from his chest, and he drew his hand up to touch the place where his heart lay, feeling it freer and looser and sadder than ever before. His heart was like that white bird he'd seen in his dreams, releasing itself finally into the open air. A horror was building behind his eyes, and then the most furious blinding white arc of pain took over in his head. He fell to the floor, unconscious and barely breathing.

thirty-nine

THEY TOOK TURNS over the next couple of days, took turns sitting or pacing in the waiting room of the intensive care unit. The usual sense of time, of hours passing, was gone from each of them. They waited in a perpetual moment of fear and grief and confusion, drinking endless cups of hospital coffee, for the five minutes every hour they were permitted into the unit to stand at Sonny's bedside in the alarming hush that hung in the air—amidst the beeping of monitors, the whooshing sound of respirators, and the quiet tones of the doctors and nurses who seemed always to be moving.

Sonny lay pale and vulnerable. A respirator breathed for him, the IV dripped into his right arm, his head was swathed in bandages. His body rested large and still and silent. Joe Rizzo had told them, after the surgery to release the pressure on his brain, that Sonny's chances of survival were "fifty-fifty. It can go either way. It's up to him now."

And somehow, somewhere in the days that he passed unconscious, somewhere in that place, that space in time where time unbends or moves differently through the body, even as his toes lay immobile when pricked, even when he responded so weakly or not at all to the doctors and nurses probing him, changing the sheets beneath and atop him, even during that time, something was moving through him. It was something he could not have named, something hazy at first, yet in those days he was floating, he was also feeling from the inside, and he began to see it all.

On November 25, the evening before Thanksgiving, the unit was quiet, and the staff broke the rules of two to a bedside and let all the DeMarcos come in at once. They stood there surrounding Sonny's bed: Rose on one side, Lorraine on the other, Dominic standing at the foot, forming a kind of circle, each with a hand on Sonny. Earlier in the day, one of the nurses told them Sonny had responded to pain and a couple of times had "tripped" the respirator. In other words, she had said, Sonny seemed to be beginning to breathe on his own and was possibly beginning to emerge from deep coma.

He felt as though he were floating, as though his body was suspended somehow above the room he was in, and looking down he could see himself in a hospital bed, tubes and bandages and strange sounds of peeping and breathing. He was peaceful, without pain, and he was waiting for something to happen. Then he felt something, like a breeze, warm and pleasant, and he turned to his right, in its direction, toward a light.

"Did you see that? He turned his head. He turned his head! He never did that before. Nurse! He turned his head." Lorraine was beside herself, hopeful and terrified at once, uncertain whether it was a good sign or an alarming one.

What was it? He only knew he wanted it, it felt good, it comforted him. He looked and saw Josie's face, serene and welcoming, her arms finally reaching out to him, and he felt happy, and she was saying, "Do you want to come, Sonny?" And oh yes, he wanted to, wanted that light, the warm breeze, wanted her to love him again, and she was saying something, something else, but look Sonny, look

and he looked and there was Rosie, brushing a cool hand across his forehead, Lorraine on the other side, gripping his arm almost too tightly, and his father touching his foot. He saw his father's roughness, the confusion in his eyes; his sisters, their femaleness warm and full of the ache he understood; his own eyes reversing their vision, moving, moving. And his heart that had lain so fragile and bruised even in this time of illness began to beat with an element of hope, in and toward himself, toward the love he wanted, and wanted to give.

And now Josephine was beginning that slight nodding of her head, and wait, he wanted her, and she was saying, "But I'm here Sonny, I'm always here." Oh yes, Momma, I know that, and he had always known that. She was moving slowly away, the motion of her eyes dark and luminous, twin suns he ached for, went from his own to looking down with him, down to the bed, saying, "It's up to you Sonny, it's up to you" and was gone. In a flash he knew he could always go, and he felt himself drift downward from floating, slowly and willingly down and closer to the bed.

"Maybe you better go now," the nurse was saying. "I'll call you the second there's a change."

He heard her say that. And realized he heard it. And he opened his eyes.

Other titles from Firebrand Books include:

Jonestown & Other Madness, Poetry by Pat Parker

The Land of Look Behind, Prose and Poetry by Michelle Cliff

Living As A Lesbian, Poetry by Cheryl Clarke

Mohawk Trail by Beth Brant (*Degonwadonti*)

Moll Cutpurse, A Novel by Ellen Galford

My Mama's Dead Squirrel, Lesbian Essays on Southern Culture by Mab Segrest

The Sun Is Not Merciful, Short Stories by Anna Lee Walters

The Women Who Hate Me, Poetry by Dorothy Allison

Words to the Wise, A Writer's Guide to Feminist and Lesbian Periodicals and Publishers by Andrea Fleck Clardy

Yours in Struggle, Three Feminist Perspectives on Anti-Semitism and Racism by Elly Bulkin, Minnie Bruce Pratt, and Barbara Smith